FREE MINTS

Hounding Prey Book 2
Listeriosis

First published by Dark Features Coven 2024

Copyright © 2024 by Free Mints

All rights reserved. No part of this publication may be reproduced, stored or transmitted in any form or by any means, electronic, mechanical, photocopying, recording, scanning, or otherwise without written permission from the publisher. It is illegal to copy this book, post it to a website, or distribute it by any other means without permission.

This novel is entirely a work of fiction. The names, characters and incidents portrayed in it are the work of the author's imagination. Any resemblance to actual persons, living or dead, events or localities is entirely coincidental.

visit my website at https://darkfeaturescoven.godaddysites.com/
First edition

Editing by H.T Fox
Cover art by Alejandro Jedrzejewski

This book was professionally typeset on Reedsy.
Find out more at reedsy.com

Contents

Preface	iv
Acknowledgments	v
CHAPTER 0	1
CHAPTER 1	6
CHAPTER 2	13
CHAPTER 3	25
CHAPTER 4	36
CHAPTER 5	47
CHAPTER 6	59
CHAPTER 7	76
CHAPTER 8	84
CHAPTER 9	104
CHAPTER 10	116
CHAPTER 11	123
CHAPTER 12	135
CHAPTER 13	148
CHAPTER 14	168
CHAPTER 15	177
About the Author	182

Preface

WARNING

This is supposed to be an uncomfortable story and does not reflect the author's real beliefs. This book contains: graphic sex, gore, mutilation, dubious consent, non consent(not between the main couple), unhealthy power dynamics, depictions and ideations of self harm. Intended for only mature readers.

For a full list of warnings, please go to the author's website and make your own decision.

Acknowledgments

Special thank you to all who helped me as a beta, editor, friend, and critiquer. Although this has taken a lot longer than was intended, I am thankful to finally have accomplished this sequel. Thank you all my loved ones for the inspiration that helped me create my series. Thanks to all who tried to bring me down so I can continue out of spite. I would not have made it without any of you.

CHAPTER 0

The sun was high and burning. Flies filled the air with a droning, deafening choir. A solitary sheep separated from the herd, twitching, sick with disease.

The creature could only jerk and drool as the rot invaded every vein in its small body. Within its eye was a nest of larvae. Squirming, eating, growing. The colony devoured the sweet matter provided by their home. What they left after their feast was bare bone.

To the maggots and disease, the sheep was their heaven. To everyone else, it was a rotting hell, and the animal was suffering.

* * *

How long has it been?
What could I have done differently?
Was it too late to call him again and make things right?
Would it even matter?
I tried to kill him. Why would he ever forgive me?

Those were the thoughts playing in Loukas Asbjorn's mind for many weeks. Even when a month had passed since that incident, he could not help but wonder how poorly he had done and how he messed up the first friendship he ever had.

Not that it mattered, he had to live with the consequences of what he was and did. There was no changing any of that.

With shears in his hands and plentiful silence, the tall man pruned his overgrown foliage that had enveloped his house in greenery. His plants littered his floors with leaves and vines to a point even he found excessive. He shouldn't have neglected them for so long, regardless of how distracted he had been.

The sounds of snipping and branches breaking filled his small apartment with a calming hum. He gave a glance to a few of his plants and determined that the potted creepers should remain as they were. Their overgrown vines looked somewhat nicer than Loukas first thought on his marble kitchen counter top.

His domain was tiny, yet it was his peace, his sanctuary. He almost felt proud that he found a place that suited him so well. A single window facing the streets covered with curtains and neighbours who cared very little about him were the biggest pros of living there. At least compared to the more lavish off-campus homes with pools and clubhouses near every bar and club in town. His home was a place of silence and comfort.

Loukas let out a sigh as he wiped the sweat from his brow, observing his now shaped-up azalea bush. For his accomplishment, he took a break on his couch and laid down on his side.

His now-longer orange bangs fell over his eyes, obstructing his already poor vision. Loukas made a mental note to get a haircut. He should not have allowed himself to get so shaggy lately. However, there still was the question of if he could make an appointment on his own or if he needed to pay someone else to do it for him.

The young man gripped the overstuffed feather pillow close to his body as he shook off that burning feeling in his gut. He needed to make a list of his tasks for today before this headache made him forget.

Breakfast

Clean

Pack

His stomach still felt so heavy from the meal of human flesh. It had been a month, yet he didn't feel his hunger as intensely as before. Even when he refrained from eating anything for days on end, his stomach only had a dull ache. It was no longer the familiar ravenous pleas for food.

Why did you eat a human being?

Why did you allow yourself to give in?

Loukas indulged in a crime to stop a passing feeling he had dealt with for years. Lust and hunger were two sides of the same coin to him. Both he could live without, and he was too weak to stop himself from satiating those urges.

Human skin, bones and muscle. That was what filled him, what nourished and calmed him. He was a monster; there was nothing he could do about it other than suffer.

Loukas wanted to suffer. He would do so with a smile on his face if it meant being a good person. A decent person.

He raised his hand to his brow and felt a sticky sheen of sweat. He needed a bath and added that to his list of things to do. Lying around his apartment was not good for his hygiene. He did not want to smell when he was at work or in class, anyway. That would draw too much attention. The idea of classes pricked him as an unsettling thought threatened to take over him.

Summer was approaching, and his stay on campus had come to an end.

He would have to go back home. Back with his parents.

Back to tell every word of what he had been doing, disrespecting and sullying their name as a degenerate.

The boy rubbed his sweaty forehead, wincing at the realisation of what was in store for him for the next three months.

Lectures.

Preaching.

Noticing he was a liar when he said he kept to their values.

They would find out what he lusted after, and what he did.

They would know.

He could not change the fact that he was packing to live the next three months in misery. He had no choice or say in the matter. His guardians were the ones paying for his current apartment, not him. He handed over all the money he made at his job to his estate. So no matter how much he hated the idea, he had to go home. He could barely live on his own, much less work hard enough to pay for his living space.

What could he do?

What was he good at?

Nothing, was his answer.

Loukas sat on his couch and gazed at the whirling ceiling fan. The repetitive motions of the blades mesmerised him. It was hypnotising and relaxing to stare at as images and memories drifted to and from his mind. He could still see that little goat beast-kin whenever he closed his eyes.

He etched the last time they spoke into his mind like stone. The scent of Hide's meat and blood, the sounds of screaming, the sight of so much crimson, and the feeling of sexual release beyond his wildest imagination. All still clear and vibrant.

He was back to their fateful night again

"Oh god," Loukas had whispered, clutching his mouth, his clothes soaked stiff in the blood of what he hungered for.

A man.

A man who was far from pleasant. Nothing more than a random hooligan that Loukas should not have given a second thought, yet he could not help but devour him. The pleasure of taking another man apart, to feel his insides at his fingertips, was perfection.

To make this all even better, Hide had come in and looked so worried. So much concern dripped in the goat beast-kin's voice, Loukas would have pounced on him at that moment for calling his name.

Hide's genuine concern would not have protected him, and eventually, the goat was underneath him. Loukas admired the little goat's brown skin with unpigmented patches, his curly fur-like hair nearly obscuring his nubby horns. Hide's stump of a goat's tail was stiff with fear of what Loukas would do to him.

Hide had seen him feeding and screamed a beautiful melody. Then his body was in Loukas' grasp. He could finally live out what he had fantasised about for so long. Right then, his dreams had come true.

Or so he thought . . .

Then Hide slapped him.

But worst of all . . .

CHAPTER 0

Hide held him.

Despite what he had seen and what Loukas had done, Hide still spoke in his usual cheeky way. As if Loukas was not a monster. As if Loukas had not caused the first and only friend he had to bleed all over the floor.

Hide's understandable hatred for him came when he woke up. Loukas was sure of it. He did not care what Hide told him. The beast-kin had to despise him for being a killer, a monster.

Instead of fighting him or kicking him off, Hide did the worst thing another person could do. He had placed his rough, callused hand on Loukas' face and wiped the streams of tears.

"Hey, count with me. Repeat after me, baby."

Hide was the worst, and Loukas hated how much he missed him.

CHAPTER 1

Weeks had passed, and nothing but bitter regret filled Loukas. It had been a month since he had spoken to Hide. Now, he had to pack everything, call a plant sitter, and go back home.

Through unimpressed eyes, Loukas gazed at his expansive collection of movies, yet none of them could hold his interest. The sun was up, and rays filtered through his blinds in an afternoon hue. Under the lights, his healthy emerald children shone in their glossy delights.

Lying around doing nothing may have been a waste, but it was better than the alternative—staring at his phone all day, eyes glued on the text messages sent between him and Hide. The back and forth trailed off to only one unanswered text.

Loukas had read them repeatedly, having no hope of any response.

Loukas: Hello

Loukas: Good morning Hide

Loukas: Is everything okay?

Loukas: Sorry

Loukas: I'm so sorry.

Loukas: Hide, are you there?

Loukas: I'm sorry I'm sorry

Loukas: Hello?

He read through the barrage of his own messages and felt knots in his gut.

CHAPTER 1

Loukas knew he was a creep and not a person Hide was safe with. It did not surprise him that the little goat man wanted nothing to do with him.

He should focus on getting the plant sitter instead of probably distressing Hide with his attempts at connecting. At least with his blooming poppies, standing bright and full of life, he could pretend they were happy to see him.

Unlike Hide.

Hide trusted him, and Loukas ruined that trust.

Loukas could not stand it any more, his thoughts in disarray. He pulled down his pants to the less scarred region of his thighs. It was him thinking with his penis that got him into this mess, anyway. Fitting if he used the surrounding area to reorganise his thoughts. His paring knife was in his hand as he found a nice, untouched spot under the older rows of his inner thighs.

As usual, it made his head feel somewhat light, but at least he could focus again. He bit his bottom lip at the sight of his injury. Dribbles of blood seeped through the gaping valleys into slow streams and flowing rivers down his leg. He may have gone too deep this time. They would probably make even uglier scars and look so bad.

"Why did you do that?"

He could hear those questions now. All would blame him and hate him for this. Loukas, maybe because of the sudden blood loss, giggled at the thought.

It was hilarious to watch how much inner sewage he was losing from a simple blood-letting. His cure was to make more wounds until every drop of rot finally left his body. It would hurt and drown out every voice in his head for once. He would be pure, healthy, and finally able to be alive as a real boy.

He slipped off the couch onto his rugged floor, still laughing at the absurdity of it all.

Pure?

Who are you kidding?

This was just a bad habit, but what could he do about it? It was all so funny watching something that would get him dragged off to for another appointment with his counsellor close up again and still provide the pain he wanted. He needed that agony more than anything. It was the high he had chased, the shame and guilt it brought. The collection of controlled emotional and physical pain was what he wanted most of all.

Nowadays, the damage he caused had left few spots for him to conceal. The pain had become his new normal, the guilt and shame were akin to numbness.

It may soon never be enough. There was only so much he could do to his body before it gave up on him.

He deserved every bit of that suffering.

Ring!

Loukas pulled up his pants and hissed at the sting of the fabric against his still-healing cuts. Maybe it was his brother calling to ask how he was doing. He doubted he could fake his enthusiasm at the moment, but Loukas might brush it off as just being tired. At worst, the call was his mother, and he wanted to drop dead rather than speak with her. Or it was his uncle and he could just fall into the daze of lectures the man would give him. He dully picked up his phone from the coffee table and put it on speaker. None of the expected persons' voices came through.

What he got was so smooth it sounded like a professional singer on stage. "Puppy? Sorry if this is a bad time, but I was worried when you never called."

That unmistakable voice of Xander spoke with such honey, Loukas felt embarrassed from receiving such undeserved kindness. Loukas knitted his brow, thinking back to when he handed out his number. As hazy as the night was, it was hard to forget or miss the handsome, confident blond. His eyes were so piercing green that Loukas wondered if they were contacts. The large watercolour flower tattoo on his chest was something Loukas shamefully could not stop thinking about. Even in some dreams he had been having, he pondered about the ink underneath that tanned skin.

"Xander! Um, I'm s-o-sorry, I—" Loukas tried to collect any semblance of composure to speak. All of his attempts were failing to hide the obvious quiver in his voice.

"No need for the formalities. I just appreciate you remembering my voice."

Loukas gripped his phone as he tried to recall Xander's name repeatedly in his mind, just to be on the safe side.

"I was concerned about you. Were you hurt back there?" Xander asked.

In a shaky, softer voice, Loukas said, "I'm fine. Oh, you don't . . . you didn't have to check up on me."

"Maybe, but I just found you adorable at that party and wanted to ask if you have time to chat during the summer?"

Adorable?

Loukas ignored the burning of his cheeks and tried to brush it off. Despite what happened to the last man who wanted to spend time with him, Loukas' life threw him another one.

This all had to be a dream.

This could not be real.

Loukas lowered his gaze to the floor as he remembered why he could not fulfil such a simple request. "I'm sorry, I . . . can't stay in the city this summer."

"Aw, why not? It's absolutely lovely here. Especially around with all the festivals and events," Xander said.

"I just can't. I . . . I don't get paid when I'm not studying. I c-can afford a bit to keep it for a few months from s-savings. But. . . I can't afford to. . . actually live in it. I don't want to stress my plants out b-by moving them out."

He heard the other man humming to himself on the other end. Then a smooth chuckle crawled through the phone as Xander continued, "You know. I would not mind you staying with me. A friend of Hide is a friend of mine, regardless of how the man thinks of me. I don't want his dear friends to get hurt."

Loukas almost dropped his phone at the sudden request. This could not be real.

"I'm not sure about that," Loukas stammered.

"Let me guess. Things are not good at home, right?"

How could he have guessed?

"What? How did you know that?"

"Puppy, I've been around. I know a lot of rich kids like yourself. Young, sad, and not much they can do about it with their current guardians. They struggle during times like this. Some people have very . . . *traditional-minded* parents, not all that accepting, if you understand what I mean." Xander sounded so sympathetic to his plight even though he may not have been aware of the full scope of it.

Loukas realised what was being implied about him and cradled his phone.

He never thought too hard about possibly being gay; rather, he tried not to think about it at all. That was never on his mind until this past year, and it already spiked his anxiety even worse than it currently was.

He already had to deal with something inside him decomposing. A thing that only wished to hurt others and grow. He had his suspicions that his family knew deep down what he was, no matter how hard he wanted to hide it. They had to have known. That may be why they treated him like he didn't belong. That had to be the reason.

They knew he was not normal, and he failed at being the one thing they wanted. A normal, intelligent, charismatic son. The gay thing would have been easier to deal with. He just had to keep up appearances for their sake, as usual.

His happiness was a privilege he never deserved, and he was okay with that. He was okay living a lie if it meant they would see his worth as their child. But his sexuality and depraved interests had combined. He never wished for any of that.

Filling Loukas' sudden silence, Xander said, "If you're scared, I can call them. I could tell them you need extra lessons off campus."

He would?

"Why are you doing this?" Loukas had to ask. What was a stranger was now going out of his way for him.

"Because I feel sorry for you," Xander laughed. "You are not the first young man I've done this for. How about a little deal to ease your heart? I need a little help around my apartment, so it's not freeloading if you're worried about that kind of thing."

This had to be a dream.

Just reject it, Loukas. Why, in God's name, would he want to spend time with you? Name one thing about yourself that is worth spending time around for. He'll see what a disgusting thing you are and hate you. Just like Hide.

Loukas' mouth felt dry.

You had a good friend already. What happened? The answer is you mauled him. You saw the fear in his eyes and loved every second of it. You wanted to fuck him

CHAPTER 1

right on the floor, whether he liked it or not.

Loukas' hands shook.

And this new man. He knows nothing about you. How long until he figures out you're nothing but a creepy, filthy, depraved monster? A week? A month? Maybe even a few days with how you are. Maybe he could see exactly what you are the very moment you step into his home.

There is nothing inside of you but an empty, rotten case being puppeteered around by a beast. Xander will find out and have no sympathy for you, as he should.

Tears welled in Loukas' eyes, and he rubbed them away with his shirt sleeve. He should reject it and go home. Even if his uncle accepted Xander's offer, there was no happy ending. Even if he could spend the summer away from it all or Uncle Ricky calmed his mom down, he would only hurt Xander. Loukas messed up with his first friend. Why would this be any different?

He only hurt people.

"Loukas?" The voice alerted the man that he was still on a call. Loukas hastily blew his nose into the cuff of his sleeve to hide his congestion.

"I . . . I don't think I sh—think I can." Loukas cursed himself for sniffling. How could he even think this was the right time to feel sorry for himself? It was for Xander's safety.

Until he learnt to keep his desires under wraps and properly suppress them, he needed to keep to himself for a long time.

"Puppy, listen. I wanted to bring this up slowly, but it seems like I have to be direct. I wish to discuss something with you." The tone was concerning to the point Loukas wanted to get away from it.

"S-sorry, Xander. But, I c-c—"

"I know what you are already and I am aware you are far from human."

"What?"

This was not in the script Loukas had in his head for things like this. Xander was supposed to be an ignorant stranger who only pitied him. He would eventually learn once he got too close what kind of monster Loukas was and that pity would die on the spot. However Xander was not following his ready made lines for this play, and Loukas didn't know if he should be comforted or scared by that.

"Puppy, that's why I want to talk with you."

The ginger-haired man was still as the words crawled through the speaker. He must have been hearing things, right? With dry lips and a parched tongue, Loukas asked, "W-what do you think I am?"

"A demon, Puppy. A poor creature that no one had ever tried to understand." Xander's voice was gentle and comforting. "So, do you wish to come over for the summer? I promise I just want to help you."

"I'll . . . think about it."

As soon as he could, he hung up and stared at his ceiling fan.

Loukas didn't know what to think any more. A demon? Was Xander joking, or was he serious? How fitting if that was true. If he was losing a lot of blood again, he would be laughing. Despite this, he could not deny how nice it was not to get rejected for once.

Loukas scrolled through his phone's gallery to catch a good look at the man he made everything worse with. Hide. Another picture he snapped when the goat wasn't looking. He was outside of the library chatting with some people, probably causing trouble. Loukas was too ashamed to confront him so, instead, took a picture. It shouldn't hurt, right? Hide would never even know he did that. Loukas was not even planning to talk with him, so it should have been fine.

Loukas sighed at the picture on his phone. Hide's curly hair, toothy smile, and brown skin were things he could not get off his mind. Yet, he had long since ruined what they had.

Loukas closed the picture and texted his uncle.

Loukas: Sir, I found a place I want to stay for the summer. I can give you his number to evaluate him.

Maybe his luck was getting better.

CHAPTER 2

Loukas was grateful that his uncle accepted his change of plans, no questions asked.

It was an uncertainty stirred in his belly for hours, but once he received the plain black-on-white message, he felt a weight had lifted off his shoulders. He wondered what Xander had said that was so convincing, but that was unimportant.

Loukas felt immense gratitude towards the person who lifted that burden. He would do the best he could to make himself an ideal guest to the older man. It was the least he could do, after all.

The drive was a short one while questions ran through Loukas' mind about what Xander's place was like. What kind of man was Xander, anyway? Loukas realised just how little he knew about him, yet he was going to spend the next few months with him.

Eventually, Loukas arrived at his destination and stared at the apartment complex located in the nicer part of the city. It was a decently decorated, several-story tall condo with a nicely carpeted lobby and interior. The walls had several paintings made by local artists, and the entire room smelled of crisp, clean air from the A/C and lavender air freshener. A young lady sat at the front desk, already offering help with his luggage, something he swiftly rejected.

Now that Loukas thought about it, he had seen this place before. The complex was on a pamphlet recommended to him as a decent place for him to live if he wanted off-campus housing. Loukas considered it, but something about where it was situated turned him off. It was in the middle of down town, and that entire scene rubbed him the wrong way. In fact, this whole decor did not exactly sit right with him, with the fancy lights and abstract art he had no clue about.

His finger rested on the call button of the elevator, giving it a light press. His thoughts whirled in his mind, arguing about the mistake he was making.

He took a deep breath to steel himself.

He could do this.

"Hello? Who is this?" the smooth-as-butter voice poured from the speaker.

"Um . . . Loukas," he replied.

"Loukas? I don't know anyone called that," the voice said, and Loukas felt his heart drop.

He could not have made a mistake, right?

Was this the correct building?

"Um, I thought you would . . . give me a place to stay."

"I don't know about Loukas, but I know a cute pet I made a similar offer to," Xander teased. "If only he would call me now."

Loukas realised he was being messed with. He sighed in relief, but he winced at what Xander implied. Was he being foolish to take a bit of offence to that? As annoyed as he was, Loukas still answered, "Oh. It's me . . . your . . . Puppy?"

If a tomato was nearby, Loukas would be mistaken for its close cousin. He did not think responding would be this embarrassing, but here he was. The speaker gave a boisterous laugh at his reply. "Of course you are, dear. Come on up, I've been waiting for hours. Your trip must have been exhausting."

The elevator opened and Loukas stepped in, already tired. It was not long before Loukas was eventually on Xander's floor, where he was immediately greeted by the smiling blond, as he was waiting by the door just for Loukas. It did not matter how composed he was because the ginger's jaw dropped. He was . . . attractive.

Why did he have to think about this now?

CHAPTER 2

Finding two men attractive might have been too much. He needed better self-control.

"There you are, Puppy, looking as handsome as always."

His handsome host was almost untouched since he last saw him. His piercing on his lips and ears shone under the ceiling light. Of course, he hadn't buttoned up his shirt all the way, which allowed all to get a good look at his well-toned chest and tattooed roses. Maybe even see a nipple piercing if they stared long enough. His tattoo snaked around his body like pure art over his chest, blooming in bright pink. Not that Loukas was deliberately looking at the chest in particular. He preferred the behind—

Stop that.

"Um . . . I . . . h-hey," Loukas said, not sure how else to introduce himself again as words suddenly seemed optional. He stuck out his hand for a shake, hoping that would be enough.

Xander threw his head back and laughed, noticing Loukas' flustered demeanour. Loukas lowered his hand, wondering if he was already being made fun of before the blond passed him a gentler smile and took his hand.

"Don't worry yourself so much. Just enjoy my place for as long and as much as you like. I fully understand if it's all still overwhelming."

"I—thank you."

"You don't force yourself, precious. It's alright."

Precious?

He was precious?

Loukas lugged his suitcase into the carpeted living room to take it all in. Carved shelves stood in the corners of the room. Within them were tiny porcelain statues of exotic animals and strange almost fairy-like creatures with their lower halves being of furry hoofed beasts and their bare upper bodies being of small chubby humans. The carpet and the sofa were a bit on the tacky side, striped and covered with polka dots, as if from another time period. A large aquarium sat in the middle of the room, shining with low LED lights to complete the strange new world he had stepped into.

What caught his interest the most, however, were the shelves and display cabinets filled with stacks of books. Some looked older than him and were wedged between the newer editions in their brightly coloured spines.

"I see my collection caught your eye," Xander whispered into Loukas' ear, causing the man to stagger backwards.

"Ah, um . . . I just see you have a lot."

Xander chuckled and moved to one cabinet. He knelt to reach the lower drawer and pulled it, revealing a collection of expensive wines. Some were in obvious French, while others were in a language that not even Loukas could recognise which further deepened his curiosity of Xander. He must have been to places that were beyond any Loukas' books and films to have acquired trinkets such as these

"Yes, I do. Some were gifts from certain people, others I bought on my travels. I enjoy reading a few now and then, but as a collection is how I appreciate their true value."

"You travel?" Loukas asked, gawking at the idea.

He was lucky enough to be outside, so the idea of outright leaving the country entirely was unreal to him.

"Yes, it's a hobby that I had a few years ago before I decided it was fitting to spend the rest of my time in the place I was raised in." He gave a wink. "I can talk your uncle into letting you travel with me one day."

"I . . . I will think about it." Loukas was not even sure if he wanted to do that, but to leave everything was something he occasionally thought of. Not like it was realistic or possible for a man like himself.

Was he being messed with again? He did not know any more.

"Back on topic. I'm more of a collector than a reader, but I never mind sharing. You like to read?"

"Um, a bit. Mostly, um . . ." Loukas allowed his gaze to wander upon the titles, one of which caught his attention, and he could not believe what he was seeing.

"Oh wow, is that *Frischer Sommer*?" Loukas headed towards the hardback book excitedly.

"Oh? So you can read German? Never thought you were the type."

Loukas scratched the back of his head. "I can speak and read quite a few other languages. It's um . . . kinda the few things I can do well in."

CHAPTER 2

Xander laughed and patted him on the back. "Then I should take you along when we travel. You could be a decent translator."

Loukas blushed and said, "I-I wouldn't say I'm that good."

"I would have never expected that type of skill from you." Xander picked out the book and handed it over to the boy and said, "You know you can read anything in my collection on your own time. I would not mind at all, and I bet you would sound lovely speaking German."

"Ha . . . I . . . th-thank you." Loukas did not know what to think of that compliment.

"Can you give me a quick little demo of what you have to say?"

"I . . ." Loukas swallowed and stammered, *"Eigentlich isst dseine Unterkunft so sc-schön. Ich weiß nicht, was ich sagen soll. Ist das gut? Bbitte sagen Sie, dass es gut ist."*

As Loukas spoke, he could only think of how nice the man was, his hand on his back, rubbing and encouraging him to keep going.

"Adorable. Was that so bad?" Xander removed his hand, and Loukas wondered if he was just too on edge.

"I . . . I guess not."

"I have a spare bed rolled out just for you. It's in the spare bedroom, but it is large enough for your stay." Xander headed towards the kitchen, leaving Loukas still unsteady.

"Th-thank you."

Loukas smiled and tugged his luggage toward the room, somewhat relieved to have some space for himself. "I don't know how I can ever repay you."

"How about some lemon water?" Xander was already setting up two tall glasses on the kitchen counter top. "I'm planning to make a few drinks. You can repay me with your time. I can tell you are already thirsty from your trip."

Loukas gave a nod. "I guess I am, b-but I wouldn't mind hot ch-chocolate today."

His host paused and Loukas began to worry that he said something wrong until Xander simply let out a light airy laugh and said, "Alright I'll boil some water for you. Who am I to not provide the best for my guest."

Loukas couldn't help but feel a little flustered by this turn of events and mumbled, "I . . . I'll unpack and get dressed when I can."

"The bathroom is all yours."

Loukas peeked into his temporary bedroom and saw a neat futon rolled out on the floor and a small pop-up dresser. There were shelves at the walls filled with a few novels and similar trinkets as the living room. It was all seemingly set up and ready for him to make himself at home.

It was all too good to be true, yet here he was, spending the summer with a man who seemed to want him around despite them not knowing each other too well. If it was a dream, he never wanted to wake up.

After folding and putting away all his clothing, Loukas went to freshen up before meeting Xander for his drink. Entering the bathroom almost felt like he was back home again. Not in a bad way, either. Aside from the impractical shag-carpeted rug, the tub was a beauty. Large enough for his body and bright white. The warm soak was just what Loukas' sore body needed, but after such a long day, he could not help but still feel filthy. There was a worsening awareness of dirt underneath his nails and blood clinging to his skin.

He was still a murderer. Nothing could or would change that.

He had to clean every inch of his skin.

Loukas stared at his now-mutilated fingertips and watched as the nails that were bitten down to a bloody stump healed before his eyes. Its memory was a now scar blending in with the sizeable collection on his body. A thought crossed his mind at how many times he could do this. Maybe it would continue until his body would become a lump of damaged tissue.

It would fit him, of course.

"Puppy, I have a nice hot cup of chocolate ready," Xander's voice called to him. Loukas sighed and drained the tub. He took out a long-sleeve pullover shirt and sweatpants to cover his body. The man was not in the mood to deal with questions.

What gave him pause was a glimpse of his back in the full-length mirror.

Sunken circular, deep red scars lined in a row were all over his spine. Eternal evidence of what he was. He knew what would spring from the veiny mounds when he indulged in his sickness. He had first-hand experience of what ripped

CHAPTER 2

from his skin when he got excited. They were there to prove he was rotting from the inside. His foulness was ready for the day he gave in, and it would burst out of him like a boil. Loukas wondered if he could cut it all off and dig it out with a sharp knife.

Xander's voice called him again, forcing Loukas to shove that thought at the back of his mind. He swallowed it all and entered the kitchen like nothing was wrong. He had to at least try being normal.

Loukas gave a sheepish smile in Xander's direction.

"That was quite a long bath," Xander said as he handed Loukas his drink.

"O-oh, I was very sweaty," Loukas tried to explain away. His usual lists of excuses.

He hoped the other man bought it, and thankfully, Xander did not press on. Loukas settled in his seat and took a sip of his beverage, letting out a sigh of satisfaction. The creamy chocolate blended into a rich smoothness that just hit the right spot.

"Knew you were the type to enjoy an excellent cup," Xander's buttery voice jolted Loukas back to focus.

"H-huh? Um, yeah, I g-guess," Loukas said, nearly choking on his drink.

"Hmm . . . How about I add a little melted white chocolate?"

"Um, okay?"

Before Loukas could say anything else, Xander took a small cup from the table and poured the creamy liquid into his drink. To Loukas' surprise, the white chocolate was poured to form the shape of a bold heart in his drink.

"Xander, it's so c-cute," Loukas gasped in awe.

"You seemed a little down, so I thought it would cheer you up."

This warmth was something Loukas was still not used to. A sweet, friendly smile that tended and grew a little seed of happiness that was for so long neglected. Loukas felt his eyes getting slightly damp.

Damn it.

Why was a small bit of kindness making him like this?

"Th-thank you."

Xander's eyes held their pleasant cosiness as he reached out and rubbed Loukas' shoulder. "No need for that, Puppy. I just find your smile worth it.

That's payment enough. I have a few things I want to speak to you about, if that's okay?"

Loukas could see sharp fangs peeking from the man's upper lip as he sipped his drink. It occurred to him just how unpleasant Xander smelled. Not unhygienically, like ash and spoilt leaves.

So much like himself.

"We have a lot of catching up to do."

"Oh, like what?" Loukas asked. He should have asked how Xander made this delicious cup.

"I know you broke that boy's nose when you left to find Hide. Did a bad number on him," Xander said, and Loukas' blood ran cold.

He tried to push that out of his mind to pretend it never happened. He had almost forgotten what he did, but now that night raced through his mind.

That night was the beginning of the end of his self-restraint. Beating down a man until he was nothing more than pulpy mess before his eyes. The only person who stopped him from murdering him was Hide.

That tiny sweet little goat. He held Loukas in his arms to calm him down. It did not matter; Loukas still killed and ate someone that night.

With a hand under his chin, the blond said, "If you're scared, I just want to say I'm not upset with your fight. I'm aware it's difficult for you."

He grinned, and this time Loukas could not unsee those sharp needle-like fangs. They were not in a mangled mess like his own mouth, but it was distinctly inhuman and dangerous.

"You . . . you don't get it, do you?" Loukas snapped before covering his mouth.

No, why did he . . .

Xander placed a hand over Loukas' scarred digits and said, "That desire you have is not the end all, be all. It's difficult, but I knew how to deal with it when I was your age."

Desires. Was . . . Did Xander experience the same thing as himself? Maybe he was also a demon? That couldn't be right. So far, the man had been only kind to him and Loukas would call it an extreme need. But help him? Xander did not know what kind of man he was.

CHAPTER 2

He may have known a bit about his aggression, but a violent man was not the same as a murderer. However, having adjacent interests was . . . comforting. Even though Xander's probably wasn't as extreme, at least Loukas was not completely alone in this.

Xander dunked in a straw and took a long sip of his drink, allowing Loukas to take it all in.

"How old are you?" was a dumb question, but Loukas could not help but be curious.

Xander laughed, "After everything, that is what you ask of me? Adorable. Forty-eight, if that's what you're wondering."

Loukas spat out his drink. "Forties, w-wow. You, um, don't look all that bad. I thought you were around . . ."

Hide's age.

Now that Loukas thought about it, he never knew the goat beast-kin's age.

"Age is but a number, Pup. Maybe one day you'll appreciate it yourself."

Loukas could not imagine ten more years, much less an infinite sea of time.

"I-I'm not sure I'm that good enough to last that lo—" Loukas said before he cut himself off, his eyes on his half-full cup.

"Puppy . . ."

Xander reached out and cupped Loukas' face, the light contact so odd against his skin.

"Give yourself more credit. I asked for your number at that party because I wanted to be your friend. I wish to help you reach your full potential."

"Fr-friend?" Loukas felt his heart thump in his chest.

Friend.

Hide wanted to be that, too, and look where that got him. Nearly killed.

Down from one friend to zero.

What if the same happened again?

Loukas shook off those thoughts. He was lonely, and Xander went out of his way to reach out. In spite of knowing what Loukas did, he still wanted to speak with him and have him in his home. Something Loukas did not deserve.

Loukas swallowed then replied, "Th-thank you. I would be-be happy to be your fr-friend."

Xander's face beamed like a burst of afternoon sunshine. "Same to you, Pup."

There was this one question that was at the back of his mind, however. "Um, how do you know Hide? Do you even know how old he is?"

"Him? He hasn't told you anything?" Xander sounded almost sad.

"No? He . . . kinda avoided it." Loukas felt off by this whole thing. Did Xander know, and Loukas was not told?

"Puppy, Hildmire is a bit of a liar." Xander shrugged. "Even if he told me, he wouldn't have told the truth. He would even pick the lowest age if he could pull it off and tell you that's his actual one."

"How would you know?" Loukas bunched the fabric on his thighs.

"Well, we used to date a long time ago."

Despite the good-natured chuckle, hearing Hide's name and "date" brought up bitter feelings.

Dated?

Dated . . .

"Oh . . . you were his boyfriend," Loukas spat out with bitterness.

"Hm? Ah! If you're wondering, I don't feel the same for him now. I have my eyes on other people," the blond offered.

Loukas felt drained and uneasy. He flopped his face on the table and groaned, "Sorry . . . I hate this."

"Jealousy? You're so silly, you know that? It was very sweet how worked up you got over that."

Sweet?

How was that sweet?

"Xander . . . I . . . I think I may be gay."

Loukas pulled his face from the table and finally looked the blond in the eye. The other man held a strained smile. Loukas bit his lower lip nervously, fearing that he may have said something wrong or over-shared.

He clung to his pendant until he heard, "I thought you were aware of that."

Huh?

"Um . . . what?"

CHAPTER 2

Xander took another sip of his cold drink and said, "I thought you were aware of this and open already."

Was it that obvious?

Xander tilted his head and continued, "But how does that make you feel about admitting that?"

"I guess . . . comforted. Nice to know why dating before was . . . not magical."

"Dated? I wouldn't have guessed that you were a lady's man."

Loukas shook his head and could not help but laugh. "N-no, no, they were all . . . arranged dates. They were nice, but I guess not for me."

"Did my ex lead to that discovery?"

Those words hit Loukas like a train. Time stopped, and he thought back to all the times he spent with Hide. His heart would hammer in his chest when he was around him, and his palms would sweat. He would giggle and laugh every time he was around the little goat. He would replay moments through his mind repeatedly.

Loukas had a crush.

"I . . . I guess, yes."

And he messed up by trying to kill him.

"Puppy, don't cry."

Loukas felt his damp eyes wiped away with a finger and realised he had been crying.

"H-huh? What?" Loukas opened his eyes to find Xander's arm wrapped around his waist.

"Puppy, it's okay."

Loukas felt uneasy being held like this, but the man's voice was silky like the creamy garnish in his drink.

"Puppy, look at me."

Loukas turned to Xander's emerald eyes. Something was soothing about them. It was reassuring and familiar.

"I want you here to help you out, okay? Just do your best for me." He held out a piece of cloth, encouraging Loukas to take it.

"R-really?" Loukas asked as he blew his nose into the handkerchief.

"Hmm, of course. You're a sweet boy."

His voice was smooth, and his hands were moving over his chest. Loukas' feeling of unease heightened from the sudden contact. The touches and how fast this was all going, something in the back of his mind felt this was wrong. That he should tell Xander to stop, but this was another person content to be near him.

Who cared enough about him right now. Why was he uncomfortable when no one else would care this much? Loukas still swiftly pulled back, and Xander began cleaning up the table.

"Well, looks like it's time for bed. I got work in the morning, and you?" The man asked, as if nothing had happened.

"Y-yeah."

His discomfort was childish, anyway; he had to just bear with it.

He smelt so rotten.

CHAPTER 3

6th June

    Xander/Alex has been a wonderful host so far. I thought he would eventually grow tired of me, but he has not. In fact, he said he enjoys my company. He likes that I'm here.

    How do I feel currently? I would say a lot better than I have been in a while.

    I was a little worried because Hide really did not like him, but I can't imagine why. He's not a bad person, a bit too touchy, but it's not that bad. He stops.

    I got a place to stay and things to do in my free time, so it has been nice.

    I would not mind spending another summer here at all. Maybe even take his offer to travel, but I know I can't leave. It is nice to imagine the possibility, though.

    Loukas left out some of his self-discovery from his journal. He did not want that part to be known to anyone else, after all. The consequences would be unpleasant, so he made it easier on himself. It did not dampen his mood, though.

    He could not be more thankful for his uncle talking with his mother about his stay with Xander. He tried to not think about how quick the man was to accept Loukas being away from home for another few months. The lack of concern for him may have stung, but it was not his main focus.

    Loukas knew his father would appreciate that he was still out of his face for a long while. Especially with what seemed on the surface to be a more mature and respectable man. As long as his family was content, then it was perfect for him. Instead of the expected noises and confusion of down town, Loukas had hours of peace to himself. Xander was usually out for most of the day, so Loukas had to keep himself busy. It had been so long since he regularly cooked for someone in the same house.

He had been doing it to provide for other students' meals and snacks as a hobby. But now, every time Xander came home from his job, the man was always ready to shower Loukas with praise and appreciation for the meals he made.

What did he do for a living? Loukas should ask him in the future.

A thing that was slightly off was how Xander's hands wandered over Loukas' body a bit too much for his tastes. Loukas wondered if it was intentional or exaggerating it in his head. His host always stopped, never seeming to acknowledge what he was doing.

Eventually, the comfort of being around Xander won over the discomfort and became a norm in the following weeks. It was just how his new friend was. It seemed like Loukas' luck was finally changing and he could relax. However, the growing feeling of hunger had crept over him inch by inch every day. It was easy to ignore at first, but it was an itch he could not quite reach and he knew it would get worse.

The feeling of satisfaction from human flesh was still at the back of his mind, reminding him of what he would love if he gave in. But he was stronger and resisted that temptation. It was what he could do to pay back Xander for his kindness. Maybe one day he would be strong like this with Hide.

The days of lazing away, however, did not last for long. Loukas, one night, lay on his bed. His eyes were in one of the many books Xander had on the shelf. A thick black leather-bound book in a fancy white font. It was a piece of literary fiction, according to the blond. Loukas' attempt to read it gave him a feeling of unease. It was a simple story about a man contacting demons. Not a subject he enjoyed, and he knew his counsellor would fully disapprove of him reading that type of book. Yet he could not help but be a little curious.

Xander told him it had a good ending. However, summoning and taming a demon was all described in such meticulous detail a sense of unease began to take hold. The main character went about his task so single-mindedly

CHAPTER 3

with the goal of obtaining a creature devoted to him, it was not something he wished to read any more of.

Loukas had to put the book down and now missed his old collection of books. He was still on *Burning Heat: Book Five*, and he doubted Xander would be interested in that kind of stuff. The man's tastes seemed odd, and he clearly preferred much older, hard-to-read works.

Loukas laid the book on his stomach as his head felt like it was in a murky haze after tea.

This was not unusual. Tea with Xander usually put him straight to bed, but this time he felt too nauseous to sip any more of his drink. Maybe that was why he was not feeling up for reading. The harder he tried to focus on the words, the less clear they seemed to get.

Maybe he needed to see the sun. He had not once gone outside since he arrived. He could not bring himself to sleep, so the man lay on his plush futon with headphones in his ears, listening to the slow, relaxing music as the minutes ticked on. Maybe he should get some water.

With his mind made up, Loukas got up and headed towards the kitchen, turning on the tap for his parched throat. He thought about a plan to store his leftovers better for the following week, only to hear the hum of the television in the other room.

Xander was up this late?

Loukas gave it some thought and decided to check up on him. Maybe he too wanted a sip of water before bed. Loukas stood at the living room door, seeing the back of the man's blond hair on his slightly tacky couch. His hair was now free from its ponytail, flowing past the shoulders limply.

Xander's head blocked the screen of the TV, but Loukas heard the vibrations from the speakers, so he knew something was on.

"H-hello?"

The other man seemed to notice Loukas' presence and turned to him with a smile.

"Oh, you want something, Puppy? Have a seat." He patted the empty spot next to him.

Loukas walked in, hoping he was not interrupting anything.

"Oh, it's nothing. I just want to know if you would like—"

A loud, lewd moan emitted from the speakers and stunned Loukas, who turned to see what was on the screen. In hindsight, it was obvious from the start, but Loukas preferred to hold on to the bare amount of decency he had. Two well-toned and oiled men were in a fit of passion on some counter top, complete with an obvious green-screen background.

"O-oh," were Loukas' only words he could muster.

"Hm? Oh, just a little old movie. I would enjoy your company, though this film is rather boring, if you don't mind."

Loukas glanced at the screen again. He did not know what kind of movie this was, but he had his doubts it was just a movie. He would ask, but he was already on edge, blushing red from head to toe.

"I . . . I . . . oh. Am I interrupting?"

Loukas may have been sheltered, but he was not ignorant of what males like himself tended to fall victim to regarding pornography. He had tried to avoid it and had done so successfully, holding a bit of pride in himself.

What truly aroused him were too specific and awful anyway, so maybe that was a hollow victory.

He also did not want to watch porn in the same room as another person at all. Loukas glanced back at Xander in the hope the man was joking.

However, instead of hot and bothered, or like himself, embarrassed . . .

Xander seemed bored.

"So, what did you want to ask me?" Xander said, his bare feet buried in the shag carpet. Under the low lights, Loukas could see drips of water slide over his damp hair, a towel resting over the shoulders of a fluffy white bathrobe. He may have just gotten out of the shower and was naked under that robe.

"I . . ."

"Fuck, take it, you stupid slut!"

"I . . . forgot." Loukas did not want the other man to notice how bothersome this whole thing was to him.

"Hm, I guess that happens." Xander turned back to the screen. "Not really my tastes, though. Maybe it's to your liking. You are a young man, after all."

Loukas viciously shook his head. "Oh no, none. I d-don't watch stuff like

CHAPTER 3

this. N-no never. I have a computer, but I have a parental content lock on it and don't know the password, so never. Haha."

He never got the chance for this kind of thing, anyway. Loukas tried not to focus on the grunts of masculine pleasure in the background as the actor plunged his cock again and again into the ass of his co-star. Maybe he could focus on the actor's dirty white socks to get his head clear.

It certainly helped. Those things were practically filthy, and he was not sure how anyone could be aroused after noticing that. He did not want to think about how he wished it was him and Hide. The man's legs wrapped around his body as he plunged into him, hearing his moans and squeals of pleasure.

"I would say the same. Not much of a fan. Not even when I was your age." Xander chuckled.

"I . . . Yeah. I should go."

"Sit."

It could have been him, but for a second, that sounded less like a request and more like a command. He turned to see Xander's soft smile and pushed that thought away as he sat himself down.

"Okay. I just . . ." Loukas tried to talk, but the orgasm of the men in the background reached a crescendo as the actor pulled out his cock from the well-used, puffy hole. His sperm was now free to spill out and dribble onto the dirty tile floor.

"As for sex, I'm not a fan of topping or bottoming. I prefer a 'hands-on' approach," Xander said, turning back to the screen.

"What?"

"We're all gay men here, aren't we? Unless you don't know what you want. You prefer to take cock or give it?"

"N-no, I . . . . I don't know, I just was not—" Loukas hated where this was going and what was being asked.

Why were they talking about this?

"Good boy, so I can skip the sex education. Loukas, you and I may be more alike in our interests than you think." The man pressed a button on the remote, letting the CD drive slip out a disc. In his hand was another one that was completely blank except for the scribbles of a black marker on it.

"We both like to read and enjoy a well-brewed cup of tea."

Loukas was grateful the topic changed, even though he was not sure where Xander was going with this. "I guess we do a bit. Um, that's not another . . . explicit movie, right?"

The man bellowed. "That other one bored me to tears. Simple sex on-screen is just so dull. I could have that in real life if I wanted. But I'm sure this one suits both our tastes."

Before Loukas could say anything else, the screen lit up, showing a room that looked like a dark concrete basement. He was relieved it was not another porn film, but something about it made him feel unsettled. Glass shards littered the floor. It was bare aside from the old bit of tape stuck to the wall to the broken pieces of wood. It all made the place look like it had been abandoned for several years. Whoever held the camera was not a professional. His hands shook and did not help the feeling that Loukas was watching some low-budget horror film.

"Is this a horror movie? S-sorry, I'm not much of a fan. Not that it's a bad thing you are." Loukas scratched the back of the head. Xander placed a hand on his thigh, forcing him to pay attention.

"Don't worry, it gets better. Keep watching. I promise you'll like it a lot."

Gulping his water, Loukas put down his glass and kept his eyes on the screen. The cameraman's right hand was in the frame, covered in a black leather glove holding up a pair of scissors. For the next few minutes, the footage was him stumbling in the dark until a rotten door came into frame surrounded by mould-covered boxes. The door opened to another dark room and Loukas heard a low moan.

"I don't enjoy watching footage of sex, but I enjoy a more interesting display of affection," Xander said as the cameraman placed his camera on a pedestal to stop it from shaking. They adjusted the lighting and the dark room became much clearer.

In a tiny square room was a man whose ass was facing the camera, stuffed with several lit and melted candles. The hot wax caused burns on his thighs and calves. Hooks impaled his body, pulling his skin taut, lifting the man

CHAPTER 3

a few inches from the floor and revealing several damaged, bloody holes. The moans of torment that fell from his lips were haunting as they echoed through the screen. Loukas wanted to scream, look away, and tell Xander to turn it off. But he could not move; he was firmly stuck in his seat with no means to take his eyes off. The cameraman's cock was in the frame, a pierced thing with rows of studs along the length and a little hoop at the head. The gloved hand began stroking it to full mast, prepared for whatever he was planning to do.

"As suspected. Puppy, you're very hard watching this, right?"

"N-no, t-turn that off." Loukas broke out of his trance to hide his stiff hard-on. He prayed Xander was teasing and hadn't really seen it. It was a failed endeavour. Even with his loose sweatpants, the tent pitched was noticeable to a blind man. Loukas panicked. "Please, I don't like this movie. I-I . . . I'm not . . . I don't—"

Pain and agony roared through the speakers as the victim wailed for mercy. Xander licked his lips and grabbed Loukas' hand before the other man could react and tug away. His guided hand cupped Xander's erect cock underneath his fluffy robes.

"That's what I mean," Xander said. "I enjoy this too and it was obvious you love it from the very second I turned it on."

The pleas for mercy crammed into Loukas' ears when the candles were extracted. Whoever was the cameraman kept shoving them in and out. Red, hardened wax and blood ran down his perfect cheeks and thighs in almost indistinguishable streaks. If the cameraman was rougher, he could cause a nice prolapse from that puckered hole. If Xander was not watching, Loukas would have given in for just one moment and pleasured himself from the open wounds painting the body and sounds of screams from the victim's throat. It was erotic in ways he had only dreamt of.

He wanted this.

"It's sick." Loukas tried to fight, but Xander's cock under his hand made a heat fill him. It was firm and slender. He could feel some piercings along it as well.

"Hm? Now that's interesting," Xander smiled as a tentacle had slithered out from Loukas' back, leaking with thick fluid.

"Oh no," escaped Loukas' lips as he was now terrified of what was happening. "N-no, not this."

With one swift motion, Xander reached out to the squirming, excited thing and gave it a harsh squeeze. Loukas yelped as the appendage tried to pull out from his hand, but the other man's grip was too strong.

"Were you scared of this hurting me? Silly pet, listen to what I'm trying to tell you. This doesn't scare me."

Something about Xander was scarier than his urges.

Wails on the screen came to a stop once the poor man's head was chopped off his shoulders. It flopped over the dirty mattress with a thunk as its last note. The cameraman kept violating the now-deceased victim with the sharp end of a machete.

Into his ear, Xander whispered, "You can't hide that this turns you on as it does for me. When I say we are the same, I mean it in more ways than you think."

It was sensual, taboo, yet Loukas could not look nor pull himself away from the hand on his face. The older man's other hand moved over his neck down to his chest.

If he asked for help . . .

Xander understood what sickness he had yet seemed so composed and intelligent.

Xander understood him.

"I can help you. We both know no one else will understand or help someone like yourself. Most would just throw you away in a hospital if you're lucky, should this little secret come out."

The scenarios Xander described ran through Loukas' head in quick succession, all making his chest feel too tight. His pathetic waste of a life would be over; there was no question about that. As much as he feared acting out again, the possibility of someone else knowing and their reasonable hatred scared him even more. Loukas' hands were shaking as he heard his companion continue with, "As also a demon, I know what this is like."

A thin, creeping branch-like appendage brushed against Loukas' back and

CHAPTER 3

the poor jumped swiftly, turning to his host who was simply amused. What was touching him just now?

Xander laughed, but Loukas did not find that funny at all. It made his skin crawl and heart ache. He was right. His main concern now was who could help him. Right now, he could not even pull his eyes off the hot cum glistening on the open, bloody wounds of the still-warm dead body. It ran down its beaten back in a mix of milky red. If Xander was not there, he would have enjoyed himself in the exact way normal men enjoyed regular porn.

This film differed from his imagination in the worst way possible. Nothing from his mind could compete with such perfection.

In a soft voice, Loukas said, "But . . . how can you—"

"Be as I am right now? It's because, unlike you, I can control my urges." The man laughed. "It's rather simple, even though you're a bit older than myself when I started, I truly believe you can learn quite easily," he purred. "I can help you, and I know you have some much potential. You are too perfect to be wasting away like this."

Doubt was coursing through Loukas' mind, but when he heard his saviour call him perfect, that apprehension vanished.

"I'm . . . I'm perfect?"

He was wonderful, he had potential. Those were words that sounded foreign to him, but now they were said by a man who was the very definition of perfection.

"Of course, Pup," Xander leaned closer to him and this time, Loukas allowed his touch. "I rarely do this kind of thing for just anyone. All I want is to bring out your true potential so you can achieve all you could have ever desired. You don't want to be alone dealing with these kinds of things, do you?" Loukas didn't want to be alone like that. Perfection had found an opening to slip a hand under his shirt to caress hot bare skin. "So my sweet Puppy, do you want my help?"

Through a lustful haze, Loukas noticed just how low Xander's hand was going. His finger now traced circles on his abdomen.

Loukas muttered, "I . . . I would like that . . ."

With the small amount of self-restraint he could muster, he lifted Xander's hand away, slipping out as swiftly as he could, just like before. The tentacle slinked back into his body, and he stumbled off the seat onto the rug.

"I need some air and a bath," Loukas stammered.

Xander shrugged as if nothing was wrong and said, "Of course. You can get that anytime you want. Just don't break anything."

Loukas laughed nervously, and he swiftly shuffled back through the door and out of the room. All to make as much space as possible between him and Xander.

He got back to his bed and could not sleep. Instead, he pumped his cock as he remembered every scene he could from that *film*. He imagined it was him performing as the cameraman. Occasionally, the handsome victim morphed into Hide as he poured his seed into his ravaged, swollen hole.

So loose for his enormous cock to stuff.

He spilled his lust into his fist, knowing it would never compare to the real thing.

His genuine desire.

The one Xander had been with. Loukas wondered what those two did together that made Hide the older man's love. He was so confident and caring and Hide is so stubborn and crude.

Did Xander fuck Hide roughly? Slamming the goat into the concrete floor, grinding that smug face clean off?

Or maybe Xander was gentle as he cut into Hide's skin on his chest and peeled it all back to show one colour. The older man would have shoved his tongue into the muscle, flicking it as Hide squirmed underneath.

What did Hide's moans sound like during it all?

Loukas saw a glimpse of what he enjoyed again with that video; he needed to repeat his first murder. The first time Loukas indulged was the first time he knew exactly what he wanted in a man . . . His insides. They were so wet, sticky, and warm. Their innards were much prettier than he ever imagined. It was all worth it to have another mere glimpse. The next time he would repeat it using everything Xander might teach him. Everything Hide loved . . .

Loukas lay in his bed, gasping as he came down from his orgasmic high. He lifted his hand to his eye level, seeing strings of cum lacing his fingertips.

CHAPTER 3

He could not help it.

A waste of his seed.

He hated such a wasteful act, so he cared very little when his serpentine tongue lapped up the web of cum on his hands, cleansing it. It did not bother him when his tendril slipped from his back, holding his hand still so he could pretend the hand was Hide's face and he was cleaning it up.

A man Loukas wanted so badly yet knew he couldn't have.

Loukas was back in reality again as the guilt threatened to consume him once more. He lay there staring at the ceiling and what he just agreed to do with Xander.

I don't know.

Those were the only words he could bring himself to jot down in his journal. He kept his gaze on the ceiling, hoping it collapsed on him.

CHAPTER 4

Hide knew Loukas was a monster. A horrible beast who devoured another person right in front of him in cold blood.

That freckled face of a timid church mouse that seemed so harmless to him was a killer. To think Loukas was supposed to be one of the millions of faces that would come in and out of his life, popping into his memory sporadically until finally drifting away like dust.

But he did not fade away, and Hide could not help but tease the timid man whenever he could or more accurately, bully him. At first all Hide did was insult him, intentionally flustering the boy with vulgar words he knew Loukas hated, throwing balls of paper at the back of head just to see if he would notice. The boy took it all with nothing more than a weak wince and incoherent words under his breath.

Not once did he ever raise his voice or fight back. Loukas was an easy target. Despite this, Hide had a soft spot for him. The boy would always bring him food, even though he never asked. Loukas would ask him how his day was, even when Hide had not been polite or had done the same, and listened to him and seemed in awe of how smart Hide was. It was enjoyable hanging around him, though he probably thought pain killers were the equivalent of heroin.

Loukas was a sweet, tender-hearted man in ways Hide always noticed.

He could have easily killed me that night.

CHAPTER 4

Hide thought Alex had something to do with this. It was the most unsettling thought he could muster regarding that incident.

Alexander, that nasty tool who always wanted his way. A sleaze willing to entice someone at their most vulnerable and get them to do whatever he liked. Hide could still remember how it was when he was with that bastard.

The man spoke so sweetly to him on the awful night when he had escaped that horrible monster he lived with. His elegant hands held Hide and offered him a better place to stay. Supposedly, it was where the beast-kin would be safe and able to build a new life. Hide was too naïve at the time and accepted an offer too good to be true.

It was another mistake he would always regret.

Loukas' aggression had to be Xander's fault. But it led to other questions, such as what that man had to gain with Loukas. They could not have spoken for long, so it was unlikely Alex could have learned enough to be interested. He also doubted the ginger was all that interested in the man, anyway.

Looking back on it, Loukas had always been a fixated stalker before he met Alex. That stalking was of his own volition, not anyone else's. Now Hide was back to square one with his questions.

Why did Loukas kill and eat another man?

What was he?

The sound of paper slamming against the table brought Hide out of his musings. Carole's stoic eyes scanned him as he laid on that beat-up old couch.

He gave her his usual devil-may-care smile and said, "Eh? You know I ain't reading any of that shit."

He leaned back into his muscular fox friend, giving him a nudge in the ribs.

"I know. I just like the sound of paper against the coffee table." Once again, Carole had to be passive aggressive about things. If only she would just insult him directly for once.

He hoped there was not a quiver in his voice to give away how agitated he was.

He witnessed a murder and did nothing.

The brown-haired fox did not take it as a joke. Instead, Makhi said, "Shouldn't you go to the hospital or something? Your stomach looks really bad. It's leaking something."

"I said I'm fine," Hide snapped. "Just got a little injured when Loulou went a little too nutty and got out when I could. No harm, no foul. I'm fine."

"I would normally agree with you being so lively right now, did you even clean the wound? It smells infected," Carole said as she poured him a cold glass of water.

"I think she means if he got that violent with you, shouldn't we get the police involved?" Makhi picked up his cup and gave Carole a nod of gratitude. "That guy sounds terrifying."

Hide rolled his eyes. "First, the boy's probably rich as hell if he's at that school. His old parents can sue us all to the ground several times over. Second, fuck you, I'm fine. You don't gotta shove your pity crap onto me."

Hide regretted what he said as he noticed the fox pull away, making an aggravating situation even worse. He, of course, swallowed that pain as he tried to focus on the major topic at hand. He could not tell them Loukas killed a man. Nor could he tell them that Loukas attempted to cut him up like butcher meat.

"So I shall sit here and do nothing else," Hide continued with a full chest of renewed stubbornness. At least it resulted in the annoyance and groans of his companions..

The fox beast-kin male next to him grimaced at the stack of papers present.

"Come on, really?" he said as he shuffled through the many pages. "So why am I here if you are that insistent on not doing anything? Aside from borrowing my printer and teaching your room-mate how to use it."

"Hide has little patience with explaining anything to do with computers. Your help was more than enough," Carole said.

"I don't bother with old ladies." Hide huffed. "If you can't even turn the damn thing on, why in God's name should I bother with you?"

If he wanted to waste his time he would rather do it watching paint dry rather than teach someone that ignorant.

"Point taken," Makhi said with a weak smile. He would tell them both to screw off if they wanted to waste his time.

"This petition is just a precaution. In case you want to file a restraining

CHAPTER 4

order and—"

Hide sank into his seat. "I said I'm fine. You are not listening to me. I don't need any of that. I don't need a doctor or the police or the damn money-sucking lawyer."

"Hate to break to you, but that guy was stalking you for a year. We kinda are a little worried about you right now. That shit I heard makes people go missing." Makhi placed a hand on Hide's head and the goat wanted to lean into his touch.

"I know, I know. It's not like I don't get that," Hide sighed. "You guys know I hate pity, alright? I don't need that now."

Although he did like it when the ex-soldier was this worried about him. It was so rare, but he craved that kind of concern.

The fox's affection, however, was platonic. It was what one had for an old school buddy and Hide needed it. He needed that affection so badly it hurt. His heart ached all over even worse than the poorly-stitched wound on his stomach.

"Alright." The fox threw up his clawed hands. "Still, you ain't going back to that guy, okay? He seems unhinged."

"As if," Hide muttered, laying back on the couch. "Wouldn't be caught dead around him."

He hated how hollow his statement sounded to him. For some dumb reason, he empathised a lot with Loukas. Something haunted the man, and he was obviously bottling it up. Hide knew what that was like. When he thought too hard on things of the past he felt ill. A lot of those memories were connected to Alex, and the feelings of disgust tainted even the nice memories they shared. He just had a life of abuse with nothing to show for it.

That was all he had other than the clothes on his back and the shoes on his hooved feet.

He liked to think it had made him stronger, but he always felt so weak. Freedom was what he desired. He would give up everything to have had that from the start. Makhi no longer spoke to his biological family for a good reason and Carole had nothing. They were both doing well. Hide should have been the same as them, but not once in his life had he felt he had control over anything.

Makhi went to the army and shaped himself up and got away from it all, but it cost him his leg. Carole went into teaching, and it led her to discover alcohol to cope. However, they had some control, some stability.

He had nothing.

"So now what?" Hide grumbled as he shifted on the couch, his ears flattening and eyes glaring at the ceiling. Hopefully, he did not space out too long this time.

"I guess we're not gonna call the cops any more." Makhi shrugged, much to Carol's barely hidden disapproval.

Hide rubbed the healing bandaged wound on his stomach and let out a feverish sigh. He'd had to replace that thing three times so far. Each time, the yellow fluid seeped like a leaky pipe. He could smell a pungent odour of a putrefying corpse.

Carole turned on the fan for him, his reasoning was no other than being hot. He just knew it felt nice to his increasingly sweltering skin. The sting on his stomach was ever present, burning and throbbing. All he wanted to do was curl in on himself, but he did not want any of these people asking questions.

What if they took him to the hospital, and the staff started trying to get in his personal business? Perhaps the doctor would try to remove his clothes by force when he told them to fuck off and not touch him.

Hide didn't need that. He never needed that, so he just needed to wait it out. This would not be the first time he had gotten sick and would not be the last. He just had to grit his teeth and bear it.

"Fuck cops," Hide said, dripping with bitterness, "they'll give me a drug test or something and then jail time. Use your brains, people."

"Sorry," the fox said, rubbing the back of his neck.

"Any opposition?" Hide added.

Carole sighed. "You are too stubborn . . . As long as you don't stay around Loukas, I guess it's fine."

Hide buried his face in the patchy cushions. His joints ached.

"Good, now let me sleep on your ugly couch. I'm tired."

CHAPTER 4

"Hide?" Makhi asked, oddly worried. A treat to hear.

"I said let me sleep."

The goat man groaned and let out a sigh of relief as Makhi placed a damp, cold towel on his forehead.

"I figure a hospital would just lead to a refusal," Carole said, but Hide did not care as she placed one of her decent blankets over his body.

"Fuck no, I'd rather die," Hide murmured.

Maybe it was the fever, and he was talking gibberish, but Hide did not care. He just saw a man kill and eat someone and it both scared and turned him on. He just wanted these jerks to let him sleep and not think about the next day.

They listened to his request because the next time he opened his eyes, he was lying on the couch alone, an ice pack on his forehead and a fan on his body.

Hide grimaced in the darkness, already feeling worse off than he did before. Gross and sweaty was not a combo he enjoyed. His throat felt dry, but he felt too weak to leave the couch. Or so he thought until he spotted a glass of water and a white pill next to it on the table, most likely left by the woman of the house.

With a weak, limp hand, he picked it up and wondered why she bothered with this.

Hide took a sip and tried to collect his thoughts. Carole was a loser and annoyed by him and vice versa. All they had between them were dull chores and dull pleasantries without even the benefit of a fuck buddy exchange. She was certainly a lady because he would never understand what went on in her dumb mind.

Now that he thought about it, what happened at Loukas' apartment was so surreal. It was as if he was watching a TV show as an audience member, safe in his seat. But blood caked the floors and his shirt, and his body ached and stung.

Hide raised his hand to his face and felt the sticky sweat and dried crust from his fever lay over his body like a thinner second skin. He really should take a shower, but his legs felt too wobbly to hold his weight. Resigned to his fate on the couch, he remembered when he tried to have sex with Makhi last night. He tried so hard for weeks to hide his injury, but it was not enough. Hide could remember the look on Makhi's face when he saw what was on his stomach.

A nasty bloody wound.

Makhi had been concerned for him.

"Dude, what the hell happened?" the fox shouted as he backed up on the bed.

"Come on! I was so close." Hide was on his knees. He had imagined the man inserting his fingers into his poorly stitched hole to open it as he came.

That was how he even got dragged here. If things were different, he would have tried to get on the fox's bad side, as mild as it was. Hide would have aggravated Makhi enough to hurt him. If only the fox was vicious enough to choke Hide out and then fuck him while he was unconscious. Just so Hide could feel the sparkling cracks of love.

Makhi was too much of a decent person.

Hide, in contrast, was a piece of shit.

Dragging his oldest friend to his nonsense. Makhi was scared for him and what Hide was doing to himself. Hide wished he were the opposite. Loukas, that red-eyed man, would hurt him and care about him in his contradictory way. No matter what Hide had done, Loukas was obsessed with him.

Hide lifted his shirt to see that ugly, poorly stitched-together wound neatly concealed behind a fresh set of bandages. Neatly may not have been the best word. It may have been previously neat, but it was now caked in itchy scabs. The moonlight shone through the curtains and allowed him to see the repulsive sight. Leaky pus oozed out from between the tiny gaps of the soiled bandages.

It painted what once was a lone creamy white patch in a sea of brown skin into a canvas of burgundy, black and gold. Worst of all, there was a faint, unpleasant odour, similar to rotting meat filled to the brim with maggots ready and their eggs squirming and pupating within the liquefied necrotic flesh. The entire area on his pudge throbbed and ached. Hide was sure he had an infection. He had tried to ignore it for a month, yet here it was.

Loukas nearly killed him.

CHAPTER 4

That thought ran through the goat man's mind over and over.

The pain racked through his body and tore him from the inside. Worst of all, his cock stood up at the thought, the image of how close he was to death. All Loukas had done to his body and all the things he could do were on repeat in Hide's mind.

With no hesitation, he reached into his briefs and began stroking his erection at the memory of being pinned down. Those large hands, that were usually so gentle, were now tight shackles that trapped his arms. It was difficult to breath with his chest trying and failing to rise with that heavier body pressed against it.

Hide grasped at his cock, biting his lip to prevent the bubbling moan from escaping his throat at the images that formed in his mind. He had tried for a while to keep his mind off such things, but now he simply couldn't help himself any more. No one else had ever satisfied his more taboo interests like that. Maybe except for one horrible insect of a man.

That annoyance of remembering an ex's name was swiftly overtaken by the more arousing memory of what that boy could have done to him. Loukas' hands, his teeth so sharp and ravishing. They were such a perfect collection of large knives in the boy's mouth and the end of his finger tips. All ready to tear into his helpless restricted body.

Hide let his mind wander to the time he was watching the sleeping man before he escaped from his apartment as quietly as he could. He rubbed one out before he left. It was so difficult to resist. A what-if scenario played out where Loukas stirred from his slumber at the noise Hide was making from jerking off.

Hide panted softly at the thought of being caught and slammed to the ground. His dick pulsed as he allowed his rough, calloused thumb to toy and tease loose foreskin and slit, dribbling with pre-cum.

It would not have been the first time someone woke up to catch him so aroused. But Loukas was different; he might even get turned on enough to kill him, and Hide would enjoy every second of it. It was just so very hard to have self-control.

Hide's prick throbbed in his palm as he could feel the man's hand in his stomach again. His lazy strokes picked up in pace. A repulsive idea entered his mind. He rubbed his fingers over the poorly healed flesh and covered it in the purulent slurry. He casually allowed his hand to roam to take in the results of his encounter with Loukas. A crusty edged, leaky wound was the boy's present to him and Hide loved it. With his hand sufficiently coated, he used this foul mix of pus and blood to aid his strokes that now flew over his length. It was somewhat ironic his annoyance of that cut not healing meant little compared to the pleasure it enhanced.

Hide, already missing how it felt to touch his wounds, used his unoccupied hand to slip under the bandages and explore the weepy pinkish white surface. Then with his finger nails he dug into it, scraping away whatever progress his body made to fix itself. He broke down into louder moans from both the pain of the intrusive rough appendages and the overwhelming pleasure said pain brought to him. It felt even wetter now, maybe he re-opened it again and it would be just like how Loukas seemed to like it. Hide could only throw his head back into the couch's armrest in the ecstasy his injuries brought to him. He arched into his hand the more he scraped into his wound, using fingernails as tools to aid in its expansion of it. He needed to go even deeper,so he could envelop his digit from its tip all the way to his knuckle. He was already gonna cum from just the thought of such accomplishment.

He wanted those tentacles to squeeze his nipples until he cried out to stop. Even in Hide's lust-addled mind, he was only brave enough to use even larger and more effective objects instead of his finger.

Loukas' passion would be addicting.

Hide moved his finger in and out of the still disappointedly shallow flesh crater, just as he knew Loukas would do. The blood he recently drew was however minor compared to the ever present slimy, rot-scented fluid was the best lubricant he had ever tried. He imagined Loukas with his smile full of sharp teeth as they grazed Hide's bare, presented neck. His soft lips would press against his skin, giving it a teasing, sensual nip.

Then he would *bite down*.

"Fuck!" Hide panted as he ejaculated into his hand. Cum soaked his shorts as he exhaled in satisfaction.

CHAPTER 4

He let out a yelp as his final jab sent a final shatter shock through his core. He swiftly removed his hand to catch his breath. A hazy thought of the ridiculousness of getting himself off on escaping death crossed his mind. It made him even hotter, but he was too tired to care much for that.

His activity coated both hands in his fluids; one milky hand smelled of familiar musk, the other deep red with slime and something foul. As usual, the logical part of his mind came back and screamed at him for his recklessness. The fact that he was fapping about such a much younger man who could kill him may have been too far. Even worse, how easily his masturbation session on Loukas' bed could have only ended badly if he'd been caught.

Makhi and Carole showed concern about him and they were right about not having anything to do with Loukas.

Hide never thought he would feel guilt over this. The memory had made him so horny it drove him crazy. A depressingly funny experience.

This was not normal. Carole told him this before, so maybe it was for his betterment to leave Loukas alone. He saw the boy's text messages, but he knew he was not the man who could be there for Loukas. He just had to let it fizzle out. It was only a matter of time. Eventually, Hide wouldn't be able to stand the boy and he would fade like everyone else.

He was just glad Carole would not know about the mess he made. Hide hobbled to the bathroom sink, clutching his lower half already planning to wash the probably stained fabric in secret. The goat beast kin winced as he took off his shirt ready to take care of his mess.

"How the fuck did this..."

It was as if he never touched it. The site was still a pinkish white surrounded by a nasty crust, but it was still unharmed. That nasty fluid still seeped out and Hide would still have to change his bandage, yet not a drop of blood was in sight.

He gawked at the thing turning to his hands to see they were still covered in his bloody, weepy, semen covered mess. Yet his body acted as if what he had just did never happened.

Hell no, he was not going to go crazy in the middle of the night on his watch. Hide swiftly washed his hands under the sink and replaced his bandages, all the while trying to not think about how he was probably cursed. For good measure, he held his head under the tap and let the cold water flow over his head.

The little goat cared little about the mess he was making in the bathroom. He didn't need to get scared or panic or make it obvious something was wrong. Stupid questions from idiots about whether he was okay was the last thing he needed. Hide's bleeding may have been only in his head, but his darker cravings were real.

CHAPTER 5

—⋄⋄⋄—

"You have not been wasting your time while you're there, correct?"

Loukas sighed at the rough voice on the other end of his phone.

It had been a while since he had a phone call with the older gentleman. As nervous as talking with his uncle made him, he just wanted to speak with someone at the moment.

Anyone.

"N-no, of course not, sir. Xa—Alex has an extensive library for me to read, and I've been taking care of myself so far." Loukas wanted to leave certain aspects out of his uncle's grasp. It was for his own good. Loukas knew the moment he even implied what Xander showed him, it would be over. Not something worth risking his stay for.

"As long as it gets you out of the house to socialise with what seems like a decent man, it should do you some good. From what he told me, he seems to have an impressive background in engineering."

Engineering?

Loukas wondered what Xander said to his uncle to make himself seem so appealing. How much of it was lies compared to the truth? All Loukas did was call his uncle and gave Xander's number. A few hours later his uncle went from reluctant to encouraging about Loukas' stay with him.

Loukas' uncle continued, "It took me an hour to convince your mother that it would be to your benefit. She's still hesitant, but your father was happy."

Loukas heard a pen click in the background. A part of him wanted to tell his uncle that he felt certain things had gotten worse since he left. Maybe Loukas still had a vain hope that his uncle would show a prickle of tenderness or concern. But deep down, he knew better. After Loukas killed his dogs out of hunger, his uncle's pity and obligate concern vanished and never came back.

"Since you haven't got into any trouble, I would assume you have been on your best behaviour so far," his uncle said. "Your journal, since your last review, showed you were keeping on track. Aside from a few distractions."

"Yes. I have." Loukas felt warm hearing that praise.

Please say it again.

"Good, I was worried you may have gotten yourself into something with how you were acting during the holidays," the older man huffed. "Just always note your responsibilities and image you need to hold up when the time comes."

"O-of course I will, sir. I will." Loukas wanted to tell him a few things. One of them was how he slipped up and killed someone. How his mother was right, and he was a monster.

How his uncle's fear and distrust of him were all correct, and he had gotten worse.

How much he wanted him to continue the scolding . . .

Yet that was nothing more than a fantasy. He said nothing about any of that and simply fidgeted in his seat.

"Anything else you wish to share?" Loukas could hear the other man's lighter click. He wanted nothing more than to beg his uncle to keep talking. Loukas wanted to hear him so he could spill his guts about all the horrible things he had done.

All he could say was, "No . . . nothing, sir. I'm alright."

"Good, be on your best behaviour. I don't want to check your arms again."

Loukas squeezed his thighs at the thought.

He hated how this made him feel.

How could he be like this?

He murmured an agreement and then ended the call before he could say

CHAPTER 5

anything else.

Loukas lay on his bed, already feeling the weight and shame all over him, accompanied by a heat in his body that travelled lower than it should have. No, he would not jerk off at the thought of his uncle praising him for his good behaviour. He was already a degenerate; he did not want to be more of one.

He picked up his phone again and scrolled through the texts he and Hide shared. They were all short and to the point on his end, unlike Hide's messages, which were filled with emotes and obvious sarcasm. Loukas wondered what could have been if they stuck together for longer than they did.

Maybe they would have . . .

His stomach growled, but he still did not want to eat.

"Puppy? You okay?" Xander's voice came from the living room before the man walked into his room and, to Loukas' surprise, held an arrangement of strawberries and fresh bananas on a neat little platter.

"I . . . I'm fine. Just tired," Loukas said, surprised by the present. Though surprised, Loukas was grateful that Xander stayed around and checked on him. Especially when he was usually out the whole day. Loukas was not sure how he could face the man after that incident in the living room.

"I got a little something from work and thought you may need something to eat."

Loukas clutched his pillow to his chest and watched as the man's fork pierced a few bits of fruit. The prongs broke the thin skin and buried themselves into the strawberry's flesh.

Loukas shook his head and said, "Don't worry, I'm not hungry."

"You're never hungry," Xander said. "I'm asking you to eat."

Loukas swallowed. He did not want to upset the other man, regardless of how uncomfortable it made him. So he stiffly opened his mouth and allowed himself to be fed.

Smiling, Xander carefully placed a single strawberry into Loukas' mouth and said, "Bite down."

He did as requested. The blast of refreshing sweetness instantly hit Loukas' mouth as he bit into the fruit. However, Loukas could not bring himself to enjoy it. His tongue told him it was a sweet treat, yet his mind only tasted nothing. He still smiled and nodded his head at the offering.

He chewed, noticing Xander attacking the platter himself, enjoying the little fruits with gusto. He did not blame him; it looked amazing and probably tasted amazing to anyone else. So he felt ashamed about not enjoying it as much as he should. A question then popped into his mind, given how much they are supposedly alike, how could Xander even eat?

"Something wrong?"

"Oh, n-nothing I was just um thank you," Loukas said, swallowing that brewing inquiry. As much as he desired to learn more about his new friend, he didn't wish to over step so soon. The last thing he needed was to come off as pushy or a bother to the person who wants to help him.

"Don't mention it. I want you to keep up your strength as much as you can." Loukas noticed a flash of suspicion in Xander's gaze before he picked up the empty plate and asked, "Do you want to watch a movie with me?"

Loukas, although on edge, was not sure what to think of such a request. He could not say he disliked the idea.

But if it was that "film" again . . .

Xander must have noticed his obvious hesitance, and he laughed. "Oh no, no, it's a regular film. Your choice. I've found a few Blu-ray discs that may be to your tastes. You can pick."

Loukas relaxed a bit and got up from the bed. "Um, sure. Just show me what you got. I would not mind if it's just a regular film."

It turned out Xander was telling the truth about what he had. The selection was phenomenal, and Loukas could not believe in his eyes. All were older films, but it did not change the fact that they were romance or fantasy classics. But his choice was obvious. The movie he picked over all the other options was *Where the Wind Blows*. Not the best book-to-film adaptation, but he could not deny he was happy to see the actors on the screen.

With popcorn, the two men watched the whole thing from beginning to end. There was not much talk between them either, but Loukas did not mind that. Just being able to watch in peace was as enjoyable as he thought it would be. Seeing his favourite moments in live action brought excitement. He noticed Xander was smiling throughout the whole thing.

CHAPTER 5

Eventually, the credits rolled and Loukas realised just how much time flew by.

He stretched, feeling a bit tired. "It's getting kinda late, but that was nice. Thank you."

"No problem at all, but I have a favour. I want to ask you, if that's okay?" Xander said as he got up. "It's nothing too big. A request."

"Hm? Oh, okay."

"It's a self-control exercise I was telling you about. All you have to do is hold a camera tomorrow morning, understand?"

Loukas had almost forgotten about this deal, but someone willing to work with him made it a situation he could not refuse. He swallowed when he remembered how easily he failed when confronted with violence.

Although uncomfortable, he had to do this. He did not want to let Xander down.

"I'll do my best," he said as firmly as he could.

"Excellent, I have it in my car and will drive us first thing tomorrow morning. So get all the rest you need."

He left Loukas alone for the night, who tried his best to fall asleep. Many questions arose about what Xander's exercise would even entail. Not one reason made much sense, and they all filled him with anxiety.

What was he planning?

Would this even work?

How would it work?

He had one guess, however, and he shoved it down. Even with that thought and the fact it was so obvious what was happening, Loukas knew he would still go, regardless. It was almost funny pretending that he didn't know and would act appalled at what they would be doing. He couldn't pretend any more; he was tired of doing that. Loukas was almost excited thinking about it. His mind raced with ideas of what he would do alone, able to indulge in what he denied himself for so long. The only time he had been this excited was whenever his uncle was ready to take him on his annual hunting trip as a boy. This time, however, Loukas was a man—a man with needs. And now, he was ready to act upon them in all the ways he had imagined.

He was sick.

Eventually, the sun rose, and as Xander promised, they prepared for the trip.

Loukas wanted to drive them, but Xander insisted Loukas sit by his side and relax. The older man also told him that once they arrived, just hold up the camera and follow him.

Never stop filming, no matter what.

Not wanting to argue, Loukas just resigned to follow the instructions. With the camera in his hand, Xander took Loukas into his car and drove off. Together, they left the prestigious down town in its glamour for the more destitute districts that Loukas was still equally unfamiliar with.

It was just as degraded as the last time he saw it. Everywhere he looked, there were potholes, trash, and construction projects that never got completed. Loukas felt a dry lump in his throat as the residential buildings towered around them and the abandoned industrial warehouses grew more numerous.

Finally, they stopped at a large, abandoned furniture warehouse just on the very outskirts of town. The door was rotten and easily pushed open as the blond beckoned Loukas inside.

"Turn on your camera and follow me. Don't turn it off," he instructed.

Loukas pressed the button as told and through the lens, he saw the room light up. He got a good look at where he was, and he scrunched up his nose at the smell.

The ceiling was leaky and so waterlogged it distended a great bit. Shattered glass, wooden boxes, and mildew carpeted the floors. The abandoned bits of furniture were either reduced to their barest parts of wood and cotton or looked like they had an infestation. Black roaches scattered over them and buried themselves into the cushions.

He followed Xander to the rotten wooden stairs that led down further into the basement as he dodged and stepped over the land mines of nails and glass. These could easily pierce his sneakers if he wasn't careful.

"I . . . What is the point of this? What do you want me here for?" he asked, as if he could not have already guessed.

He wanted to believe he was not like this. That he could be a decent person.

CHAPTER 5

That he did not want this.

"Give me a second."

Loukas knew why they were there. He wanted to deny it as long as he could.

He knew Xander made that video, and the fact he was in the same place as the cameraman in the video unnerved him. He should have called the other man out and told him to take him back home. However, he was excited.

Loukas was horrible.

They came to a room on the bottom floor, and Loukas could not stop watching. As tiny as he thought the room was in the video, the fresh addition did not help that matter. He could not help but stare at it taking up space.

On the floor was a body. No, a torso would have been more accurate. Its arms and legs were chopped off and cauterised, leaving in their place pathetic stumps that flailed uselessly. All it could do was wiggle and struggle on a dirty mattress like a caterpillar. A sensual display that Loukas didn't want to pull his eyes away from. Its tongue-less mouth could only make animalistic gurgles as it lifted its head to the two men's direction.

It was ironic given its noises were probably to get the attention of any sort of saviour. Someone who was better and not now breathing faster as he visually lapped up every inch of its damage. Loukas' increasing shame was a mere drizzle compared to his storming arousal when he saw its eyes were nothing more than bloody sliced slits that wept beautiful ribbons of blood.

He was certainly a beauty to be worshipped and admired. Watching the man writhe and cry in a sad attempt to move away pulled Loukas into the room.

"Puppy, watch me and watch me carefully," Xander purred, and with a knife, he slowly approached it.

Stop it!

Stop enjoying this!

Put down the camera.

"A reckless driver ran him over when I was on my way from work yesterday. Poor dear, no one was around, so I fixed his legs after he asked for help. My new project needed a new star. People pay a lot of money for fresh meat."

Job?

Did Xander's work involve those videos?

"Hm..."

Xander pressed his hand against the mutilated human's stomach as it tried to wiggle and thrash away. It was no use as his knife's tip teased its chest. The taut skin indented like a whirlpool under the tip until it broke and a drop of blood welled to the surface.

"Want to touch? You're allowed to as long as you can hold yourself back. His tongue is missing, so you don't have to make much of a conversation."

I should refuse.

I should...

Loukas sat near the squirming man and raised a hand to his face. The thing flinched, but Xander held the man by the waist, preventing him from running away.

Loukas stuck his finger into the sliced eye jelly up to his middle knuckle and found it felt similar to the jam of a sweet tart. Encouraged by this texture, he swirled his finger around in the socket all while the gurgled screams filled his ears. Loukas licked his lips as he felt the edges of the hole, rubbing against it and enjoying how rubbery and solid it was. *So squishy and slimy.*

"That's it. It feels so nice and wet, right?" Xander whispered into Loukas' ear.

"Hmm."

"Always been curious how an eye felt?"

Loukas said nothing; he was simply enraptured by the new toy around his finger. He always enjoyed certain textures but this was something else. It was as if it was made for him.

"Seems like you're enjoying it a lot more than you think you are."

Before he could properly answer, Loukas gave a low moan as a hand lightly pressed against the erection in his jeans.

"This hurts? Poor thing. I bet it's difficult when you don't want to touch it."

"Xander, wh-what are you—"

Letting go of the knife, Xander guided Loukas' hand to caress the terrified body, feeling it shake and gyrate.

CHAPTER 5

Without much convincing, Xander got Loukas' hand into its mouth, the body whining as it tried to pull away to no avail. The wet cave was completely different from the eye. Loukas couldn't help but prod the stump of what was once the most delicious tongue housed between slick inner cheeks. Xander encouraged him to go further and further into its mouth, tapping the back of its throat. The thin saliva was now mixed with sticky mucus coating his fingers. The man squirmed and squeaked as his throat bulged from the suffocating intrusion, before finally going limp around his hand.

That did not stop Loukas' fascination. Bit by bit, inch by inch, he could not help but explore even rougher. The familiar bodily fluid now felt mixed with something else as it coated his hand and wrist. Maybe it was blood. The throat now looked like a swollen tree stump by the time he heard a nice crack of the jaw.

Loukas' entire hand, up to his forearm, was down there now. It was nice and warm inside this man compared to the chilly basement. Like a nice, comfy hot water bottle

Loukas could only watch, fixated, as the lights of the body's most beautiful grey eyes were snuffed out. Now he was left with a lifeless meat suit wrapped over his arm. The young man flexed his hand, opening and closing, watching the throat bulge with his movement. It was a nice mitten over his hand.

It was still so hot inside of him. How long had it been since he had been able to touch the insides of another person? A month perhaps? It might as well have been years since his first time, when he had hurriedly peeled off that horrible skin layer. However, at this moment, he was fully savouring another man's insides. He didn't have to rush, and there were no neighbours for him to be cautious of. The throat was what this man used to breathe and eat. It was so fragile and so important in keeping him alive. Loukas had so easily deformed it into a mockery of its former use. All by simply pushing himself in when he was neither air nor nutrition. Could his cock be a much more suitable replacement? He could give so much more nutrition that way.

It all felt so . . .

"Hm? That was fast."

Loukas was gulping air. He had never felt more humiliated when he came down from his high. Xander casually removed his hand as if he had not done anything. He ran his clean hand through Loukas' hair to move away the bangs and placed a kiss on his forehead.

"There you are. Good filming. You enjoyed that, right?"

Then it all hit him at once about what just happened and what they just did. The stickiness of his underwear was ice cold, and he never felt more disgusted with himself.

Why?

Why did he . . .

"Why . . . did you?" Loukas felt his chest tighten as he replayed what had happened.

The other man licked his lips. "As I said, I like the same things as you do. Better this dying man than a healthy body, right? You already said you could not resist a healthy one, anyway."

Loukas' stomach knotted as if it were true.

It was very true.

"Say thank you. If you were this eager over something like that, I could only imagine how you are on normal days. You were so quick, soiling yourself."

Loukas hated himself, and he could only nod an affirmation.

"Thank you . . . Xander."

"You're welcome, Puppy. Best you clean up while I'm gone. Call me when you're finished."

Xander got up, leaving Loukas alone with his thoughts—stunned and delirious and wanting it all to end.

He did not like what Xander meant by *clean up*.

He did not want to eat anything. He stared at the body and the body stared back.

He could feel how cold this place was in contrast to the hot summer day and wanted to cry.

* * *

Loukas eventually left the warehouse and stood under the sweltering sky.

CHAPTER 5

Sweaty, tired, and in need of a change in clothes. What lesson was he even supposed to learn from this?

The only thing he succeeded at was following Xander's guidance so he would not immediately kill the man on the spot. His stomach ached at the fact that he resisted, choosing instead to spend the next few hours digging a makeshift grave. He pulled out his phone, ready to call Xander to pick him up.

The only thing Loukas wanted was a shower and bed after all he had been through. He also needed to scrape the filth off until the fire cleansed him.

That was his plan until he saw a pair of white ivory horns. He was immediately hit with the musky aroma covered in cheap perfume, a combination he could not forget.

It was him.

Hide.

It had been a month since Loukas saw him last, and right now, he had a few grocery bags full of items. He was a couple of buildings away, looking around for something.

It didn't matter to Loukas. Hide was in his sights once again.

Loukas pulled out his phone and made sure the flash was off and the sound was mute. As quickly as he could, he snapped a picture. It didn't matter, right? Hide wouldn't notice it, anyway.

Xander left without him, but Loukas could always call back. It wouldn't hurt to follow Hide meanwhile. He knew he lived in the area. The goat beast-kin's comment on multiple homes had piqued Loukas' interest.

He made sure he was out of Hide's sight as he followed, ducking in every nook and alleyway all to ensure no one knew where he was. All until Hide came to a stop at another apartment building, only slightly better than the others, and entered. It was still a mess, with its cracked windows and peeling paint. But this was another place Hide stayed. Another home the little goat crashed at that Loukas now knew about.

How Loukas wished he could enter and ask which floor Hide went to.

It would be so easy, but he knew that would be too suspicious and he already got a decent amount of pictures.

All that mattered was Loukas knew another place Hide lived. Then Loukas found something he had never been happier to find. Hide had been chewing gum and spat it out when he entered the complex. On the side walk, Loukas found the spot. Tropical punch flavoured gum. He scraped it off with his fingernail, smiling brightly. He was so lucky, especially since he found a perfect spot in his old apartment to keep a lot of the printed photos he had taken as well as mementos such as these.

If only he had a second piece of Hide's gum, then he could fully enjoy the goat's taste with one and keep the other as a purely untouched trinket.

(You're abusing Hide's trust.)

I'm sorry.

(He'll hate you, as he should if he found out about this.)

He wouldn't know.

(You're despicable.)

I know.

(Delete them and throw them away.)

I need them.

(Selfish.)

I am.

Loukas broke out of his thoughts to see a text from Xander that read, "I was wondering when you plan to get back."

Loukas sighed. He might as well get back to his apartment. He already got what he wanted.

Loukas: I'm lost. I'm on 400 Walkway Avenue. According to the sign.

Xander: I'll pick you up. It's a shame you can't go home on your own in these parts. That's okay.

Any other time, Loukas would have been ashamed that he needed help with such a simple task. However, now with several pictures of Hide's face for him to admire and his gum as a keepsake, he did not care. Xander could take as long as he wanted. Loukas wanted to spend his entire afternoon enjoying and admiring the sweet man's beautiful face.

CHAPTER 6

The corpse burned itself into Loukas' mind in the most agonising of ways. Its blood was so slick under his fingers that it felt like thick oil, and that hot wet throat over his arm made him want to shove his cock into it. He made it perfectly wide enough for himself, after all. The way its neck bulged and stretched to accommodate him made Loukas' head spin. How it struggled to move, wiggling on the floor like a clumsy caterpillar infected his dreams.

Every mutilation Loukas had inflicted on its body was an improvement in his eyes, an addition that he wanted to caress and kiss with his love.

As if to reward him for his craft, his cruelty was now his camera footage, and he could replay it all to his heart's content. Every second of the dying man's last moments were safely preserved in the palm of his hands. He did what Xander wanted and received a reward of a single touch that made him make a mess in his pants.

He wanted to bury himself like he had done the body. To be covered in dirt and not feel anything for as long as possible.

It was where he was supposed to be.

The worst thing of all was . . .

He did not actually feel guilty about killing the man. He only regretted that he enjoyed it as much as he did.

Loukas pulled out his phone and flipped through another source of his guilt, Hide's pictures. He should have deleted these but he didn't want to. Instead, he had stored some of the gum and hair he snatched into a plastic bag and hid it under his temporary bed. When the summer was over he needed to figure out where in his own place he could even keep things like this. It wasn't much room with every inch taken up by his plants. He still was nervous about who he hired to take care of them, it was better than letting them die in storage but he couldn't fully trust that they would be placed exactly how he. . .

Then a single spot popped into Loukas' mind as he recalled his apartment's layout. The perfect place for treasures like these.

Loukas lifted his head to see Xander entering his room with a cup of steaming hot black tea.

"Oh, you already had your bath? I just thought you may be a little thirsty tonight," Xander said.

Loukas had a nice bath. He needed to scrape off the filth from his skin with a steel wool. He did so until bright pink and raw scratches covered his back.

Loukas shook his head, unable to look the other man in the eye.

Xander tilted Loukas' chin to meet his gaze. "You are very poor at hiding how you feel. I can tell you're upset about something. Are you okay? I understand everything may be too much for you right now. You can tell me anything."

"I . . . I just . . . We just did something horrible to someone." Loukas finally broke as he felt his breath quicken. "We killed him. I can't—"

"Loukas, you still enjoyed it. You can't deny that."

The way Xander said his name was uncomfortable. It did not sound right at all.

"I did, but it's wrong."

"Yes, but no one is ever going to accept a man like you who enjoys this. Regardless of whether you acted upon it. You know that, right?" Xander flicked a strand out of Loukas' eyes. His hand squeezed Loukas' palm as if he knew it would calm him down. "I have a lot more self-control, but you are very different. I worry about you a lot."

Loukas clutched his pendant. He did enjoy it, and Xander was one of the few who even accepted anything like this about him.

"I . . . I know. I'm sorry."

CHAPTER 6

"I was just wondering if you were upset about that or me," Xander sighed. "It's hard to tell with you, Loukas."

"N-no, of course not. I'm not." Loukas lowered his gaze to the floor. "I . . . Can you not call me Loukas? I'm fine with the . . . the other name."

He could not believe he said that, but he disliked how the man said his name. It was so cold and unfriendly that he would rather be called anything other than that.

Xander patted Loukas on the head, moving his hand around his ear. "It's okay. It's alright, Puppy. I promise to be the one who does not care about what you are, unlike everyone else. I will always find you perfect the way you are."

Loukas did not believe it, but to hear that and get comforted like this by the much older man was a treat he would devour to its fullest.

It was what he always wanted, but never thought he would have.

"Thank you."

"Your birthday is coming up soon, right?"

Loukas, still nervous about the change in topic, gave a nod. "Yeah . . . it is."

"Good, just give me some time. And take care of yourself for as long as you stay with me. Okay, Puppy?"

At the return of his nickname, Loukas breathed a sigh of relief and nodded. "Y-you don't have to do anything for me."

"But I want to."

There was still a question that rested at the back of Loukas' mind.

"Xander . . . why are you and Hide . . . no longer together?"

Xander's smile was strained and Loukas almost regretted asking until he answered, "Because Hide does not like to do what is best for himself and never changes. There's nothing more to it. You were his friend, so you probably already know how he treats those around him. Leaving you behind was simply horrible."

"It was not like that. He—"

"Slept with two other guys while you were downstairs." Xander tapped his empty cup. "He was very talkative when he dragged you outside afterwards and word got around fast. I don't want you to get hurt by him."

61

Hide was not exactly the best person in the world. Loukas was not blind to that. He had spent a good few months as a target of his insults and horrible attitude. He was aware of all of that, yet . . .

Loukas could not be mad at him nor hate him. Getting left downstairs enraged him, but he was not mad at Hide specifically. Those two men were the problem. If only the beast-kin would let Loukas be the only one in his life.

Loukas was quiet and Xander patted the man on the head and said, "But you are the adult here who can think for himself. So this was just a forewarning. I want you to be careful, okay?"

The door closed and Loukas was once again alone with his thoughts. He understood Xander's concerns, yet he still held no hard feelings towards Hide. Neither of them was all that good for the other, anyway. Both dealt with each other horribly. And he was fine with that.

His phone began its obnoxious ring again and just as he was about to ignore it, he saw a number he never expected to see again.

With a shaky hand, he immediately picked up his phone. His heart thumped in his chest with anticipation of the caller on the other end.

"Hey? Loulou? How's it going?" that nasal voice drawled from the speaker. All Loukas wanted to do was savour every second and each syllable from the man's words.

"H-hey," the stunned man replied. Loukas was prepared to unleash all his questions that had been building up for weeks. However, the sheer volume of them paralysed him.

What could he say?

What did he even want to say?

The other end made it easier and broke the ice himself. "So, has summer been treating you right? Hot as balls out there."

Of course, that was what he would say first.

"I'm sorry," Loukas blurted out.

They could not continue like this. As much as he wanted to pretend and go along with Hide, he could not act like it all had never happened. He hurt Hide, and Hide saw him kill someone. If the goat was going to pretend for

CHAPTER 6

Loukas' sake, he didn't want that.

"I-I know you probably don't . . . don't want anything to do with me, and I—" Loukas gripped the sheets on his bed. He was just happy to hear Hide's voice again, regardless of the high likelihood of his rejection.

"Dude, quit it." Hide was firm. "I'm the one who should be sorry for ghosting for who knows how long and not doing shit about it. I'm fine right now. Does that make you happy?"

"I still hurt you."

"Loulou, stop it. You can have your pity party elsewhere. I'm saying I don't care and I don't give a shit, so you better accept it, Shark Tooth."

Startled at the sudden forcefulness, Loukas nodded and stammered, "Yeah, I will."

"I miss you, okay?" Hide said. "You and your freckled face."

Hide missed him? Even after everything?

"I miss you, too. Every day I've missed you."

"*Tsk*, yeah. Look, let's just leave this sappy shit on the ground and talk about something fun, alright?" Hide was probably practically grinning from ear to ear on the other end. "You know, how about a make-up pic of my Halloween costume last year?"

Loukas clutched his pillow to his chest. "N-no . . . I don't th-think that—"

Loukas blinked as he found a message sent to his phone.

Confused, he opened it up, and he saw . . .

Hide in a tight and skimpy devil costume. A tiny spandex speedo leaving little to Loukas' imagination. He wore the smallest tank top, a head adorned with red horns to accompany his real white horns, and a cheap plastic tail on his ass. He struck a mischievous pose on what looked like some dirty patched-up couch. Overall, an image Loukas could not take his eyes off.

The text was, "Halloween make-up gift ^_^? Do religious nuts even like Halloween?"

No, he shouldn't celebrate that, but Loukas pushed aside that thought. Hide had no idea how much this was affecting him. Already Loukas froze, watching and admiring the other man's perfect skin.

A consensual photo for the collection, something he had always wanted and now he harboured it on his phone. It was the grand prize of his gallery, better than anything he had ever taken before.

"Th-thank you," Loukas whispered before he covered his mouth. He did not want to appear like some creepy, desperate pervert to the man already. Especially after weeks of not seeing each other.

If only he could pleasure himself now with only this picture, he would in a heartbeat.

Would Hide like that?

He might have to face the goat's disgust and berating while masturbating and listening to his voice on the phone.

"*So pathetic, can't even control yourself to the sound of my voice. Sad loser virgin boy.*"

He heard that delightful laugh on the other end. "I guess you're a man of excellent tastes. I'm glad you liked it."

Loukas averted his eyes from the pic. He knew he could not concentrate if he drooled over it for too long.

He would have all the time in the world later, anyway.

There was something strange about Hide's eyes in that picture, the more Loukas focused on it. They looked tired. Where was this picture taken, anyway? Hide lived with multiple people. Some might not be good people.

Loukas said, "Y-you don't have to do that."

"And? I wanted to. I'm sorry for being a shitty friend these past few weeks."

"You did not k-kill and eat a person. You're better than me."

Hide went eerily quiet. Loukas nervously was about to ask if he had done anything wrong until he heard Hide speak again.

"I'll keep saying it. You are too fucking naïve. I'm not a good person, dumbass."

What?

"Hide, you have b-been good to me for the last year. I've . . . You're my first friend."

"Damn it, you're sappy. Yeah, and you're an alright guy most of the time." Loukas heard some soft murmurs on the other end of the phone. "Yeah maybe. Fuck, this is awkward. Eh, I'm bored now. Where you staying?"

CHAPTER 6

The swift change in subject concerned Loukas. If Hide did not want to open up to him now, it was okay.

"I'm at Xander's."

"What!" Hide shouted and Loukas lowered the volume.

"Um, yeah. He offered a place to stay and—"

"Loulou, that guy is awful, the absolute worst. What do you gotta pay him to stay? Money? Sex? Either way, tell him to fuck off with any of that. You owe him jack."

"Wh-what? No, nothing, nothing at all," Loukas cradled the phone. Hide's reaction was harsh, yet there was this agitation laced in his words. "Hide?"

"So you're just spending your time at his place at no cost?" Hide exhaled, as if he was holding back something.

"Yeah?"

"He hasn't asked you to do any weird shit, right? Or did anything funny with you?"

Loukas was about to tell Hide the answer to that question, but he stopped himself. Hide had just forgiven him for nearly killing him. Just because he said he did not care the first time did not mean he would accept that Loukas loved it and was continuing his perversions. What kind of person would like someone like that? Loukas didn't want to hurt or lose Hide, so his activities with Xander remained private.

Until the day he could stop being like this.

"Um . . . no."

"Took you a while to respond," Hide grumbled. "Just know, no matter what, I won't be mad, okay?"

"I . . . Okay."

"Baby boy, you're too easily worried about crap. It's okay. We're still friends, alright?"

It was not enough; Loukas was simply happy to know that Hide was still there. He felt his heart thump in his chest at Hide's admittance of enjoyment, and it made him want to hold on to the feeling and never let go.

Baby boy.

Hide called him that name now, of all times when the picture already worked

65

him up. Loukas inhaled sharply at the name.

The things he was imagining at the moment were too tempting. Maybe Hide would call him that again. His hand would trail down his body, noticing just how needy his baby was.

Loukas looked at the text message to get a good look at the image sent.

Smooth skin and bright eyes accompanied by his usual confidence, yet an undercurrent of sadness. Hide was the most beautiful rose Loukas ever laid his eyes upon.

He lost a bit of his shame and licked the picture on his screen and tried to imagine it as his beautiful flower among the weeds. If only Hide would touch him right now.

But he was fine like this.

His crush was simply a magical idea which would never come to fruition. Loukas was content with that. Just having Hide as a friend was enough.

His genuine desire was Hide, as a pretty rose for his pleasure to look at but never touch. Loukas, however, didn't want to nurture or tend to it as he did with his other plants. On the contrary, he wanted it to grow into a flower that only a disgusting person like himself deserved. Something putrid and rotten that was defiled in every possible way. It still looked so pure despite Hide still associating with something like him.

Loukas should have been happy, and appreciative that such a person was still by his side. Loukas, however, was selfish and hated it. It only meant that Hide did not belong to him. The goat could come and go, in and out of his life as he pleased and Loukas couldn't bear that. He needed to make sure Hide wouldn't ever be able to leave him again. The only thing holding him back is that hesitation in his heart. Outside of fantasies, there was no moral or ethical method or reason Loukas could use to convince himself that what he wanted to do was right.

This current status in his life had to be enough.

"Loulou? You okay?"

"S-sorry. I sound like a loser, right? Haha." Loukas tried to laugh it all off as his hand slipped under his waistband. He was already hard.

"Hmph, maybe. You are a loser, just the few I enjoy being around. So there's

CHAPTER 6

that."

"That's k-kinda mean," Loukas could not help but smile on the other end.

"Whatever. Anyway, about that pic I sent—"

"P-please, don't m-mention it," Loukas fumbled as he tried to cut the other man off.

"A very odd way to react to a picture. Got any plans for it tonight?" Hide teased. "A little date with rightie or leftie?"

"It's difficult already, Hide."

"I can help with that, you know."

Loukas wanted to ask him to repeat himself, but Hide immediately followed up with, "So, what are you wearing?"

What kind of question was that?

"Um . . . night clothes?"

"Hehe, I was expecting no answer, but whatever. I'm just here nude, so my nips are chilly as hell right now."

Nude.

As in *naked* nude?

All Loukas ever had of Hide were little peeks of bare flesh, never the full show.

Loukas unintentionally palmed his cock through his underwear before he heard a sharp sneeze on the other end.

"H-hide?"

"Huh?"

"What's wrong?" Loukas asked, alarmed.

"Nothing. I got chilly nips. Also, I'm not gonna judge, but I feel I may have called at an inconvenient time," Hide said.

Well, yes.

"N-no, it's never good. Bad. It's fine, the time is fine," Loukas stammered.

"I know you want to jerk off right now. It's pretty damn obvious with all that rustling in the background," Hide replied flatly.

He knew?

"I . . . I . . ."

"This is far from my first time calling a guy during that," Hide continued.

Loukas wanted to crawl into a hole and die. It would have been a blessing if he could. He heard the other man mutter something away from the speaker.

Hide was probably going to hang up because Loukas had to make it awkward.

"Loulou, I know you are gonna beat yourself up over it. But, it's fine."

It was not.

Then Hide said, "I can beat you off instead. I wasn't joking about that."

Loukas only stared at his phone as Hide began texting him.

Hide: Hey, Loulou?

Hide: Bean pole!

Hide: Tall and sappy! Come on, don't leave me hanging!

As Hide's texts flooded his screen, a part of Loukas wondered if he was having another one of those awful dreams again and he would wake up sticky, hot, and guilty.

Hide: You're still there?

Hide: Loulou.

Hide: Loui <3 <3 <3

Hide: Loukas?

He should have said no and ended the call right then.

This was all too much. It was beyond his comfort zone, and he knew he could not handle it. Loukas could so easily hang up with just the touch of a button.

But, he did not.

"I... I wouldn't m-mind," was what came out of his lips instead of a refusal.

"Cool! It's just a friend thing, alright? So don't think too much about it, okay?" Hide laughed on the other end.

Friend thing?

"I... What are y-you t-talking about?" Loukas asked, then it occurred to him what Hide was implying.

Hide probably saw sex as nothing more than physical gratification. A complete detachment from anything emotional. His casual view of it was not something Loukas could ever understand, and he did not know exactly how to feel about that. He wanted this to be so much more than a friend thing.

CHAPTER 6

A romantic notion was what his heart craved. It was clear in his mind. But to be with the little goat in any way was something he desired too much to refuse.

All he wanted at this moment was for Hide to make him cum.

"Damn it . . . forgot you're probably so virginal you piss rainbows and ride unicorns," Hide groaned.

"I don't do any of that." Loukas felt the need to correct. "I just don't know what we're d-doing."

"You sure you don't attract big dick horny horses? Shame. Anyway, let's take it slow here. For your first experience with a guy."

This was still Hide, so he should throw away the hope it would be . . . classy.

Loukas heard the man clear his throat before a purr rolled out of the speaker. "Loulou, if I were with you right now, I would be more than happy to give you a good, firm hand. I bet you're a very big boy. An entire island in those pants. Makes it difficult to handle all by yourself. Probably need an adult to help you with that."

Loukas swallowed as he muttered, "Ah . . . I . . . I guess?"

Maybe this kind of thing was not for him. But Hide did not seem too perturbed and continued his talk.

"Loulou, don't need to be so shy. I know you always wanted to be a good boy for me, give me lots of your love. If I had a task right now, my baby would know what to do."

Loukas' hand lazily began stroking himself at Hide's words. He was good.

"You're so tall, handsome, and just so obedient in everything you do. Loulou, you probably can't wait for me to touch you as you tug on your cock. You're so perverted to do everything a firm man tells you."

"Y-yes," Loukas panted.

Hide chuckled. "Keep rubbing, but do it as slowly as possible. I don't like fast shooters. You're too needy already. I prefer you to work for it."

Even as his praises turned to teasing, it fanned a flame within Loukas. He would have normally felt shame, but something was exciting about being on the phone pleasuring himself to all the things Hide offered and promised.

He did as instructed and slowed down his strokes to an agonisingly slow pace. His grip was so loose just to please Hide. Loukas felt his head grow light with need as he whimpered at how tormenting it was to be so out of reach for pleasure.

"So Loulou, baby, what do you want? You're not allowed to touch the tip until you admit it." Hide's previously jovial voice, although now stern, dripped with arousal.

Was he touching himself, too?

"Bite you so hard," Loukas finally admitted through a poorly disguised moan.

"Bite? Where? I'm simply helpless right now and you're ready to blow, all because I gave you a little attention."

"Hide, y-yes. It's . . . C-can I go a bit faster?" Loukas tried to rut into his palm.

Hide must have predicted that since he ordered, "No, don't move. If you do that, you should stop stroking. Disobedient perverts don't get rewards. Hope you enjoy holding that hard cock."

Loukas let out a whine as he stilled his body. His cock throbbed in his hand, but he could not do much more.

Hide laughed. "You wanted to do so much more to me. You got hard while we were on the rooftop last year, right? Probably wanted me on my hands and knees. My cute, perky ass is all for you."

"Those s-s-soft lips. I want to tear them off as I stick my tongue into your throat. Taste inside you," Loukas whined into the phone.

His head felt so fuzzy that he did not care how much he fumbled over his words. He just wanted him.

"My soft lips? Well aren't you a romantic. Through my torn neck hole, I'll gurgle your name, Loulou. Such a naughty thing deep down, aren't you?" Hide laughed. "For a nice reward using your adult words, you can drift your hand slowly while I'm talking. Does that game sound fun?"

Loukas could barely form a sentence as he grunted into the speaker.

Hide continued. "I want you to hold me down as you fuck me too hard, like the horny, desperate little virgin boy you are. I'll bleed over your cock to make it all easier for you to slip in and out of me."

CHAPTER 6

"I want you . . .," Loukas begged, "so much I want to see you bleed."

He was already more than pent up from before and knew he would not last much longer with the lewd words pouring over him, no matter how slowly he went. He wanted to do so much more.

He desired to hold the man down and rail him until he screamed for mercy. He could see Hide's eyes swim with lust for him. His legs would wrap around Loukas' waist as he pounded into him, making Hide his.

His neck would bear a permanent scar of his love. His perfect body was suitable for the perfect, sweet soul within him. If Loukas could not rot his insides, he could taint Hide on the outside to be just like him.

A tendril rose from his body to grasp his cock to assist his hand. This should have disturbed him, yet Loukas couldn't bring himself to care. Why had he been denying this pleasure? He allowed the tentacle to pleasure him slowly, imagining it as a hole he could penetrate.

How would Hide feel being marked and defiled by a corpse like himself?

He would fill Hide with his dead seed as it burrowed into his ass. Its sickness that had cursed his own bodily fluids that Loukas desired to spread. His gift would swiftly spoil Hide's once pure, untouched blood into vile sewage. Once red would become a pitch black sludge; its purpose would be to spread Loukas' rot into every part of the beast-kin's body, corrupting it from the inside out. Organs would melt together in an undistinguishable mass as their purpose was now altered, and something else would keep the little goat alive now. Every part of him would be full of Loukas' decay, marking him eternally as his.

The tendril, now slick with his ooze, pumped him with ease. Even toying with his slit, making Loukas wish it was the other man's tongue.

"And I will be yours, baby. My blood and my body are ready for you. You can cum now, Baby boy. You can go as fast as you want. Let it all out."

Instantly, the tendril went faster, and his hips moved into its strokes. It was as if they knew his exact likes more than himself. They wrapped themselves so tightly around his cock, squishing it to a painful flatness, simulating the tight hole of the one he couldn't touch.

His hand still shaky held his phone to his ear, and he cared little for how perverted he sounded as he breathed out heavily, "Hide. . . You're so… I want to fu-be in you so much."

His now-free hand moved to his chest, caressing the sensitive skin, imagining it as Hide's hands touching his body. However, it wasn't enough. It was big, too soft, and he couldn't bite into it for its divine red wine. This would never be enough.

With a desperate cry, Loukas' hips jerked into the slimy appendage. He spilt over his stomach and bed sheets, coating it in a sticky mess. He rode his orgasm until he spurted out one last dollop of semen and then collapsed in a limp heap.

It was hard to tell how much came from his cock or from the tendril. All that mattered was it soaked his sheets and shirt and he'd clean them later.

Loukas' head whirled from satisfaction. He panted as he basked in the afterglow.

He heard Hide let out a sigh as he most likely reached his peak himself.

With little thought, Loukas muttered into the speaker, "Thank you."

A pathetic response, but the man on the other end did not seem to mind it. Instead, he laughed and said, "Haven't done that in a while with someone. Normally I'm more up close and personal, but this was fun. You need to work on your sex talk, though. Maybe one day you'll make a man want cum with just your voice. You're sweet, so you got that going for you."

Loukas vaguely wondered if Hide was aware of what he would have done if they were up close and personal. However, his normal anxiety did not come to him. He was too emotionally exhausted to dwell on it or the internal guilt and shame.

He nuzzled into his pillow and grabbed a box of tissues from his bedside table to wipe away the mess on his abdomen and sheets. It was not too effective. Even when the thick goop was no longer present, the large blotches of wet spots remained.Out of courtesy, he changed the sheets and lightly washed them before any possible stains set in. Loukas stared at his hand to see it still covered in his seed. With his long tongue, he licked his digits clean. If it could not be in Hide, he should at least save it for later. His tongue and body would revert once his excitement died down, so he might as well enjoy

CHAPTER 6

it while he still could.

"Shit, I'm tired," Hide mumbled on the other end, pulling Loukas out of his daze.

A question, however, occurred to him.

"Why were you up this late, and what are you doing right now?" Loukas asked.

There was a pause.

"Not stuttering as much, huh? Never knew the cure for speech shit was fapping together."

Could he not make things embarrassing?

Then it dawned on Loukas...

Hide does this when he is avoiding something.

"I... No, I mean, I'm just worried about you, since... you don't have work right now at the university due to the break. I just want to know if you're safe or... doing okay."

Hide returned his question with silence. Did he step too out of line?

"H-hide?"

"I'm fine. I wanted to talk to someone. Someone nice, I guess. I've got a headache and coming down from some sketchy stuff, but I've been worse and better," Hide admitted in a soft voice.

This concerned him. Wherever Hide was, Loukas could not help but worry about him. He did not know or understand why the goat was the way he was. And probably neither Hide to him. Maybe he had no place to have a say in it, but he could not leave Hide alone like this.

"Um, I want to b-be there. I mean, I'm available 24/7 if you... want to talk."

"Shit, you know I still feel like crap for ditching you for months," Hide admitted. "You're a good kid."

"I wouldn't say I'm that, but I—"

"Ugh, stop with throwing back my compliments." Hide sounded exasperated. "I fucked up and no, I don't care if you went Hungry Hippos on me. Don't care, so take my compliment."

"I—"

"Candy Cane, take it."

"Y-yes, I'll . . . take it."

He heard Hide snorting on the other end. "Good. Another thing, although I'll believe you about Alexander not doing anything fishy, I'm saying best to get out of there. That guy's a creep."

"B-but he's been so nice and friendly so far." Loukas didn't want Hide to get the wrong impression. He gave into his depravity, not Xander, and he could not let the man take the fall for his illness. "He hasn't forced me to do anything I didn't want."

"Sheesh, I guess you're on defence for that fucker." He heard Hide sigh. "Fine. Look, you're an adult. I'm not gonna force you to do jack. Even if he's not forcing you into anything, just know I'm here, okay?"

"Okay."

"Boo, this is boring. Let's change the topic to something more fun after our little hiatus." Hide reverted back to his usual cheer.

Loukas pulled himself out of bed, and with his remaining courage, asked the simple question.

"D-do you want to spend some time together . . . this summer somewhere?"

Loukas' anxiety gnawed at him until he heard the response.

"Maybe. I normally stay at Carly's place, and Makhi is usually busy. But she's boring as hell, so sure, I'm bored. I'll think of a place later this week."

"Th-that's great. Um where are you at the moment?" Loukas tried his best to hide how much he wanted to jump with joy.

"I kinda lost her keys tonight, so I'm staying with some other people for a bit. It's just cold and gross, but I'll be fine."

That did not sound nice at all.

What more could Loukas even do?

He had a feeling if he offered Hide a place to stay, the goat would reject it outright.

Loukas, taking note, replied, "Okay. I'm free most of the time. So if you have an idea, I'll be available."

"I bet you are, Twig. Also, thanks, Loulou. Thanks for asking."

"Don't mention it."

CHAPTER 6

The call ended, and every emotion crashed all over Loukas.

Had he made a mistake?

It was too late to regret that for now.

Loukas lay awake in his bed as he tried to list what he was supposed to do.

He made Hide happy.

Hide thanked him.

Hide did not hate him.

(*But when he learns how much of a freak you are, he would wish you were dead, like Mother.*)

I know.

(*Good thing he's a lustful thing cus you would have touched yourself to his photos tonight as soon as he got off the phone.*)

I still would.

(*There's no saving you. Deep down you love that he's the mess he is. Easy way to sate your perversions. You like him like this, don't you?*)

And he'll never know me. I will never let him know.

(*Pathetic.*)

Because I am.

He listed what he had to do on repeat as his mind fell asleep.

Wake up . . .

Do not masturbate to his picture collection.

Not touch himself to the memory of his first friend's voice.

Clean Xander's apartment.

At least he can do two things right the next day.

CHAPTER 7

Alexander was a horrible man, and Hide wished he had never met him. It had been years, but Hide could remember like it was yesterday. A fake smile, white teeth, and a gentle voice that so many would fall for.

Even when they first met, Hide felt uneasy around him and could tell he was faking some of his niceties. However, he was just as foolish as everyone else back then. That day was cold and wet. The goat had no raincoat to keep him dry as he sat at the bus station, unsure where he should go. Hide had neither a coin in his pocket nor a crumb in his stomach, and he did not want to go back to *that* house. If he were to starve or die from exposure, he did not care. Both were preferable compared to living with that old man.

He was an idiot to trust someone like that.

The little goat was aware he may not have been the greatest kid to foster.

Too cold.

Too excitable.

Doesn't focus.

Not bonding.

He did not think he was that bad, and yet, no one wanted him. Maybe it was being a beast-kin that made those undesirable traits worse to potential guardians. To some humans, they were just slightly above animals. They were to work the land and do the more laborious jobs that were too dangerous for most humans, or at least that was what his uncle told him when he asked

CHAPTER 7

about it.

Beast-kin were either prey like sheep, goats and rabbits, or predators like foxes, lions, and wolves. Prey like him were considered easier to manage, weaker, and submissive, while predators were unruly, stronger, and unwilling to back down. It was blasted all over his file to get someone's attention, and he hated it.

The staff saw him as a pet to be advertised to a couple wanting a cute creature they could coddle. Hide was not delusional enough to hold out hope for other beast-kin wanting him either. His distant attitude along with his other "behavioural problems" put a lot of potential parents off.

His long list of food intolerances should have been the straw that broke the camel's back. A herbaceous diet made his limitations worse that not even milk could go down his throat without him vomiting. No family wanted to play Russian roulette at every meal.

At least Makhi had such a chipper attitude that no one seemed to mind the canines and claws. Maybe they also thought he was ugly.

It did not matter in the end. Only one person eventually wanted him to stay long term.

Hide wished the staff had never allowed it or believed all the lies he said to get him.

It was almost funny. When he met the man, he found Hide too cute and wanted him to stay once he aged out of the cute difficult child appeal and into a still-difficult-but-not-so-cute pre-teen. Hide should have been suspicious, but at the time, he could not be happier.

He lost Makhi around that age. The fox had his own family, and he was old enough to stay with them despite their own host of problems they had. Hide was alone, so it would not hurt to make a friend who wanted him, right? No one would know. It would just be between the two of them.

Messages sent between Hide and him beforehand were always more on the mature side. But it made him happy. He was not a dumb kid and was just so mature for his age.

The man comforted him when a girl who was not all that interested in continuing after their first time ended. He was there when Hide vented about classes.

It was a one-sided friendship and Hide fell for it every step of the way.

He grew to hate those greasy hands.

He was old enough, after all.

Mature enough.

For years.

It probably did not affect him that much because no teacher noticed. Not that it mattered. He would not have told those nosy, self-righteous bitches anything.

In the end, it never mattered. His memories of their time were too poor, and all he could recall clearly was that the man loved to smoke. Most of those memories were gone for better or for worse.

Eventually, Hide left after losing a fraction of his boyish looks and voice. His birthday reward was a bloodied nose and a limp from his attempt to steal everything that monster had.

His only regret was not doing it sooner.

Hide sat in the rain wondering where he was to go now. What could he even do?

The voices were the few things he remembered.

"Who did this to you?" Alex had asked, his brow raised. His face was so cold. Now that Hide remembered it, he seemed more curious than concerned with him.

Hide panicked and tried to scramble to his feet. He did not want to fight, but if he had to, he would not go down so easily.

"Get the hell away from me. I'll bite your fingers." He had struggled to get up, and Alex just watched him.

Hide remembered his green eyes. They seemed more amused looking back on it.

"You're hurt, and that wound on your leg looks infected," Alex said. "Come on. You can stay at my place for a bit. Unless you'd rather get arrested for loitering."

None of the options sounded good, but what choice did Hide have?

Alex grabbed his hand and Hide accepted. The goat was too tired to fight

CHAPTER 7

or argue with the man. He was just relieved to find one person who cared enough.

Alex was a person he loved and could not stand after he realised the horrible piece of shit he was. Now Loukas, a boy Hide somewhat cared for, was staying in his home. Hide had no idea what to do about that. He could order Loukas to stay away, but the boy defended the creep so earnestly it made Hide's skin crawl. Why hadn't he noticed how close those two were?

He really fucked up.

Hide's memories and regrets flowed through his mind, pouring out the images and scenes. He lay on the couch staring up at the ceiling, holding an ice pack on his black eye.

Even now, not a lot had changed. Men were still ever so rough about what they wanted.

Age did rot a man.

He wanted to poke at the bruise, to make himself shudder in the contradictory pain, but he decided against it. *Not in my house* was her rule, and he was not ready to break it in broad daylight when she could walk in at any moment.

Hide's gaze turned to the table, where a half-empty cup of water and some medication sat. Painkillers were the only drug allowed in Carole's apartment, as if he would not try to steal the over-the-counter medication to sell or use.

The rule was stupid anyway. Every time he used to come over to Carole's place, there was more than enough in his system to hold him over.

However, he felt drained, tired, and sick. Being sober sucked, and he hated it. He was nauseous and on edge whenever he thought about his life. He should have gotten over that years ago, but he couldn't. Why couldn't that pain die already?

He was stronger than this. He'd been through worse, so he just had to suck it up and keep going.

The lowest point in his life was behind him, and he should move on. Alex killing that man should stay in the past, and Hide shouldn't even dwell on it.

That was no longer working. No matter how hard Hide tried, flashes of old memories kept coming back. Even now, after all these years, he was sick when they entered his mind. He felt eternally forced to relive a nightmare. Drugs helped drown it out before. Now he was not sure what he could do other than ignore it and hope it went away.

He wiped his face to remove any evidence of wetness from his eyes. Remembering his injury, Hide lifted his shirt for a quick peek at the cut. The previously unhealed wound was now a clean scar that ran across his stomach, with no sign of its previous infection or abnormality. It was rough to the touch, yet felt so soft and sensitive. Hide pulled out his phone to check the time. 4 AM, too early. His mind was buzzing, and he was not sure if he could sleep much, anyway.

His ears flicked to the sound of a fridge opening.

"Who goes there?" he said, knowing damn well who it was.

"You're up already?" that monotone voice of his friend said. Hide saw the black-haired angel approach the living room couch, a bottle of some cheap beer unashamedly in hand.

"You kept the ice packet on. Surprising," she said. "Thought you would toss it as trash."

"Well, it hurts and I want this to stop swelling before I go outside," Hide said. "I don't like being asked stupid questions."

"Lovely. I'm not much a fan of scraping you off my doorstep again. Keep it on," she said. Hide kept his gaze away. It was not the first time this kind of thing happened. "Hide, you'll eventually get killed."

"Don't care," he snapped.

It all was the typical series of events. He ended up pushing his limits a bit too far and needed somewhere to recover, which was frequently on her couch. Not too different from how they first met. Him jumping out of a dumpster he was hiding in and caught her off guard.

"You—"

"If you stopped drinking so much, I would consider your opinion worth my special attention," Hide grumbled. "Mrs 'rules for thee and not for me.'"

She was quiet and Hide didn't feel apologetic. If she was going to critique his life, she had better been able to back it up with her own.

"Good night, Hide."

CHAPTER 7

As expected, she avoided the topic. As far as Hide knew, she was too forgiving beneath her cold facade.

That was why he hated how she handled things. She was supposed to be better. Much better than him, same cloth, but who had got it all together.

Maybe that was why they had always put up with each other.

Realising she would leave him alone in the dark, he quickly changed his tune.

"I talked to Loulou yesterday," he called back.

That thankfully got her to pause. She returned and sat next to him.

"Why?"

"*Tsk*, I dunno. I just felt like I wanted to. He's a dumbass, but we talked things out and stuff."

"Didn't you say he almost killed you?"

Hide threw his hands in the air. "Oh, come on. It's not like I'm doing anything wrong here."

"Never said that."

Hide glared at his friend. Her gaze was, as usual, stoic, but there was a hint of annoyance at his accusation. But how could she get off judging him?

"Yeah, but I feel bad for him, alright? Just been a bit stuck lately, so I was wondering if he'd chat."

Carole tilted her head. "Don't you have Makhi to talk to?"

Hide laid his head in her lap and sighed. "I know. It's just . . . nothing's going anywhere. Nothing budged, nothing changed, and I'm tired of it. I'm sick of waiting for something to happen. He hasn't exactly been a fan of some things lately."

"You like him."

"Yeah, I guess." Hide scowled. "Why do you give a shit what I like or don't like?"

"Pity." He appreciated the honesty at least. "And you're not a completely intolerable man," she said.

"I don't want some drunk's cheap pity. Acting all better than me when you're a freaking loser who thinks feeling bad for me makes you a god or something."

Hide immediately regretted his words as Carole immediately got up, and without her ever looking him in the eye, he could tell she was at her limit.

Her harsh words said more than enough. "Good night, Hide."

Hide wanted to call her back and say he was sorry, that he did not mean it and to stay with him a bit. Even for just ten more minutes, he just wanted someone by his side. But the words stuck in his throat, and he just sat where he was.

He fucked up and he knew Carole would be upset with him for who knew how long.

He scrolled through his phone and saw Loukas' number.

Hide: Hey, there's a festival in town next week and I got some free time on Friday. Wanna go out or something? I'm bored as hell right now.

He was ready to set his phone aside and forget about it all in the next few days. Until he saw Loukas' reply.

Loukas: Oh, I've never been to one. Yes, I will go.

Thinking about how to respond, Hide shrugged his shoulders.

Hide: Sweet, it's gonna be hot as balls, so unless you wanna be burnt freckles, get some sunscreen, hehe.

Loukas: I guess I should buy some tomorrow. Thank you for reminding me.

Hide smiled at what Loukas replied. Even though it was a spur-of-the-moment invite, he could not help but feel a little excited. He would apologise to Carole later.

He gave that idea some thought before a better one came to his mind. With a pen and paper in hand, he wrote out what he wanted to say.

Sighing, he got off her couch and pulled on a somewhat clean T-shirt while he searched for a pair of his slippers. He might as well stay at Makhi's for a bit, anyway.

He should have never gotten so comfortable so quickly.

Dressed more appropriately, he found Carole's spare set of keys and left through her front door. He made sure he set his note on the open coffee table for her to see.

Carole, I'm sorry. I worry about you a lot and am not a fan of how much you

CHAPTER 7

drink. I know what it's like. You know what it's like, but you are a teacher. A smarter gal than most girls I know. Don't worry so much about me. I'll be fine, alright. I've been fine before and I'll be fine now. If you're wondering, I'll be at Makhi's for a bit.

You will always be a 3.5/10 girl on my scale. You know I prefer girls with more meat on them, so take that score and do what you will with it.

You're decent.

– Hide Presont

CHAPTER 8

Loukas took a deep breath as he tried to steel his nerves. As difficult as that was, he had to keep a level head.

He stood at the entrance to the fair decorated in coloured banners and artificial lights. His eyes were behind a pair of shades to protect against the high and blazing sun. He winced, raising his hand to his forehead to wipe away the sweat already pouring over his face, making his bangs stick to his forehead. He really should have got that haircut already.

Loukas tried to focus his attention on something more pleasant, like the leaves and scent of freshly bloomed summer flowers filling the air.

Balloons of an occasional clumsy child floated up and dotted the blue sky above. The wind blew the faint aroma of seasoned smoked meat that somewhat whet his poor appetite. At the entrance was a sign, hand painted by a local primary school in watercolours with the phrase, *Summer Gendon.*

Despite the horrible heat, Loukas refrained from the popular attire of T-shirt, sleeveless under-shirt, and shorts that showed too much skin. Instead, he opted for a cotton long-sleeve V-neck shirt, jeans, and sneakers. His body was too scarred for cooler clothes, anyway. He just had to make do with what he could.

The ginger exhaled as his gaze fell to his phone to check the time.

Of course, Hide was ten minutes late.

He's ditching you.

CHAPTER 8

He would not allow these thoughts to make his life miserable. He had just gotten back his friendship with Hide and did not want to ruin it with his paranoia.

Of course, Hide was late. He was always late, even for work. Loukas nodded at the internal assurance, but it still ate at him from the inside.

"Hey, Loulou!" that scratchy voice bellowed, and all Loukas' worries vanished. Here was Hide in only a vest and shorts and flip-flops. Exposing so much skin. Even his collarbone was bare for anyone to see. Or touch.

"Happy birthday!"

What?

"I . . . Excuse me?" Loukas said, confused.

"Your birthday is in July, right?" Hide leaned forward, his smile jovial as if he struck gold. "Turning twenty-one this year?"

"Yes, but . . ." Loukas refrained from correcting that it was the following week.

Hide still remembered his birth month.

He remembered.

"Um, Loulou." Hide tilted his head aside as Loukas tried to wipe the tears forming. No one had ever told him happy birthday in years. Except for his brother, those words had not once left anyone's lips as soon as they deemed him too old to care.

"N-no, it's nothing. Just a little surprised," Loukas laughed off.

No one except Hide was happy that he was born and alive. No one but him. He was the one who cared.

Hide's rough, calloused hand entwined with Loukas' palm, tugging it to the entrance. "Well, come on already, let's go! Before any of the lines become fifty people, minimum."

"Okay, okay. I'm coming."

This time, unlike last year, Loukas walked with him instead of being dragged along.

"So, um, what do I do first?" Loukas looked around at the numerous activities. From getting up and close with a band to trying free samples.

Hide stuck out his tongue and pointed towards the tents and booths.

"First on the agenda is me winning you a prize, of course. I'm kinda a prize guy and always win the best rewards. I'm just too good at this. It's a curse."

Loukas was in doubt, but what did he know? With how excited Hide was and how confident he seemed, he may have been right. Loukas watched him approach one booth with a sleepy deer beast-kin teen. The teen gave a yawn and handed over three balls to Hide for his dollar bill. Hide gripped the ball, watching carefully, and prepared his aim at the bottles. Then missed every shot he had in three seconds.

"They rigged this game," Hide stated, glaring at the deer.

Loukas picked up the ball, handed over his debit card to pay and said, "C-can I try?"

"Sure, why not? Bet you got good aim and strength," Hide whispered away from the teenager. "They're probably glued together. I just know it."

Hide popped behind him, giving him a reassuring pat on the back. Loukas felt his breath catch in his throat as the man held his arms and said, "Just relax and aim. Don't worry too much about anything and just play, babe."

"Babe?"

If Hide's goal was to throw off Loukas' attention, that nickname was the quickest way to do so.

"Yeah? And?"

Loukas felt his chest tighten. A part of him wanted to tell Hide to not call him that because it was distracting and inappropriate. Another part wanted Hide to call him that again.

"Hey, you two gonna do anything?" the teen asked, his lazy eyes on the other customers behind them.

"Hey, we are paying citizens. Don't push us," Hide huffed.

The man would get them kicked out.

Taking a deep breath, Loukas aimed and . . .

He knocked none of the bottles down; his aim was even worse.

"I can't believe this." Loukas felt so useless. Hide rolled his eyes and gave him a pat on the back.

"What if I said you looked pretty sexy back there?"

"Hide!"

CHAPTER 8

"Glad that got your attention. Come on, big guy. Stop moping. We got more places to see, anyway."

"Aren't you a little disappointed?"

"Nope, they're probably cheating, and I don't care if you suck. So let's go, the lines are getting too long."

Reassured, and with a weak smile, Loukas took Hide's hand again. "Lead the way."

The sun was burning his skin even with his sunscreen, yet that mild discomfort barely had a place in his mind with what they enjoyed at the many booths and games. From trying to win a pet fish to stopping by the arcade to see Hide's talent at Shooters Shine, it was non-stop event after event. Game after game, they wasted not one second idling.

"Hmm, thirty thousand and eighty-five jelly beans." Hide pulled his face away from the jar after one glance as the booth manager stared at him in awe.

"Th-that's exactly right, you win . . .," he said, gawking.

Hide smirked, turning his head in Loukas' direction. "Told ya this was too easy. Now pick a stuffed animal before I get banned from these types of booths again."

Loukas stared at him, limply pointing to a large fluffy lamb toy, and said, "How did you . . . figure that out?"

"Easy maths," Hide shrugged. "Loulou, the average jelly bean is around two centimetres long by about one and a half centimetres in diameter. This brand, though, seems to be smaller at around one point eight centimetres long, so—"

"I think I got it," Loukas said, squeezing the toy close to his body. He only heard centimetres and already gave up trying to understand.

Hide nudged him in the side. "Trust me, I can take all this boring ass maths shit and put them out of business. They are so lucky I'm merciful. Now take a pic of us with this stupid toy and let's go, babe. We got five other places to be."

Loukas did so with Hide posing in the picture with the fluffy toy. He snatched Loukas' sunglasses and placed it on the toy just as the timer went off. A silly picture with Loukas caught off guard squinting at the sudden light, Hide out of focus, and the lamb being the only thing clear looked ridiculous.

It was their kind of ridiculous, no one else's. As if they were just an ordinary couple. Just two men who enjoyed the games, art, and music. But, a silly thought and wish. This was not even a date, and Loukas was already comparing it to one.

Each new moment Loukas made permanent with a photo, all of Hide and sometimes himself. Loukas was in those photos, and everyone was smiling and laughing. It was something he still could not believe was real, yet it was on his phone as clear as day.

Eventually, they had to take a break somewhere and although Hide had plans, Loukas wanted to return the favour. A place he looked up specifically to give them privacy, a nice place to eat and watch colourful fishes.

Hide flopped onto the lush seat of their private booth, stretching his legs.

"Fucking hell, man. My feet. I should have worn sneakers," he said as he pulled off his flip-flops and tossed them aside. He wiggled his hooves before rubbing with his hands.

Sitting opposite him, Loukas took out the menu, looking through all the potential options they could have. He glanced over to Hide for his own input and saw the goat scrunch up his nose at the menu grumbling, "thirty-five dollars for raw fish? Are these people insane or something?"

That was not much of a surprise at this point. Maybe it was not a good idea to take him to a place he would even dream of going. What if he was already bored of this and Loukas had already ruined their day?

"I'm letting you pick surprise me baby boy," Hide tossed the menu aside with a smug smile which made Loukas' anxiety over this lunch even worse. The beast-kin trusted him to order something he would like and he couldn't let this opportunity slip him. So still undecided on what to order for himself he sent a request for the evening special. It was not long until Hide's was clearing his plate of rice balls, mochi, and avocados.

"Okay you win, you surprised me," Hide said mouth still full of half chewed food. "I guess you got an eye for this kind of thing, Cherry Boy."

Loukas nervously laughed blushing at the compliments. He didn't mind being called Cherry Boy; at least it was less vulgar or rude compared to Hide's usual nicknames. "Yeah, I know a bit about food, and thought this dinner, I

CHAPTER 8

mean lunch would be your kind of thing."

"Sounds like you've been taking notes on my interests. Trying to study me instead of your major? Hide teased as he stuffed another rice ball into his mouth.

I wouldn't call what I'm studying. I'm just observing. I'm not getting graded or tested on what I've learned though my notes anyway.

Loukas' gaze went to the aquariums of tropical fish that gave their booth the feeling of being underwater, surrounded by a coral reef.

Diver's Brook, it was called. A restaurant he spent days researching.

Something Hide said was well out of his price range, yet Loukas insisted he would pay for it. He did not want to be a leech; this was a day for both of them to have fun. The benefit of this specific place was that it acted as both a quiet hotel room and a restaurant.

Customers had their own overpriced mini bar when they didn't want to order a full meal, a hot tub, and a private bathroom. It was a choice as to whether you wanted to eat, stay the night, or both.

The whole place was tough to reserve a room for and Loukas' only compromise was getting the room that had the broken hot tub. Hide's disappointment when the staff told them that was a stab. However, it was a blessing. If there was a working hot tub, Hide would ask him questions about why he refused to take a dip. Loukas was not ready to answer that kind of question.

"You one of those foot people or something?"

"What?" Loukas, baffled at the out of blue question, had no idea what to even respond with.

"You were staring at me massaging my hooves earlier. Makes me wonder," Hide said as only taking a brief pause to swallow and then pick up another slice of avocado.

"N-no!"

"Glad to have your attention, with you day dreaming the whole day." Hide pushed away his now empty plate and said, "Let me guess, the hooves are weird as hell to you."

"Yeah—um, no. Just . . . I've never seen much beast-kin before, so I'm curious."

Hide grinned and leaned over the table. "So ask away. We got time and half since I can't eat most of the shit on here anyway? I'm a rice and garlic filled basketball right now, so I'm not moving my ass from this chair."

Loukas thought for a moment and then asked, "Um, so you can only eat veggies?"

"Kinda. I mean, I got a fuck ton of intolerances outside of that." Hide grumbled. "It's kinda why I stick to pure vegan shit most of the time. I know it's less likely to make me vomit. Milk, eggs, and fish are just nausea in food form to me. I haven't tried peanut butter cus I'm not risking it."

"Ouch, that sounds horrible."

Hide shrugged. "It is what it is. At least as far as I know, sweets and cheapo shit from the store haven't made me sick, so it isn't the end of the world. My turn."

Hide thought for a moment and asked, "So why did you pick that university in this dump of a city? I get rich fucks choose it cus it's easy to get into if you got too much money and are too dumb to get anything better. But even then, you gotta have better options."

"It's just closer, that's all," Loukas said as he poked at the table.

"Boring, that's a lame answer, Richie Rich." Hide cocked his brow. "Now that I think about it, I don't even know what family you're from, anyway. Like all these guys get some fancy ass last name in some moon language."

"Because that doesn't matter," Loukas said swiftly.

"Why?"

"Cus it doesn't."

"Why?"

Normally he would worry about the attitude changes that people underwent when they learned about it. They would start treating him nicer and asking more and more questions. Never did they wish to learn about him, his age, his likes, his dislikes. It was all so shallow what they wanted to talk about with him. Usually, they ended up asking about putting a good word in for them and getting his father involved in their political campaign with funds. Or their daughters, sisters, nieces that would adore meeting him. Their words

CHAPTER 8

and smiles never matched what their eyes told him. They only wanted one thing.

Hide, however, brought on a fresh fear Loukas never thought he would have. Hide was everything his family stood against. They were outspoken against beast-kin like him, layabouts, heathens like him.

Hide might not want to deal with the son of the company who funded programs telling him he was scum. They were usually under the guise of good intentions, like informing of drug abuse but then warning of how beast-kin's are the ones that encourage it. Or how more funds to churches that preach of them having no souls, were just a branch of life akin to animals.

Another secret he would rather bury within himself.

Hide was not letting go. "But why? Don't leave me hanging."

Loukas sighed and shook his head. "I don't want to."

Hide was in thought and said, "If it's because your folks are shitty, I don't c—"

"They're not," Loukas corrected.

"But why are you staying with Alex, of all people?" Hide took a sip of water. "Most rich kids who aren't taking summer classes usually go right back home on whatever holiday they got planned."

Loukas never really understood that. If they had the ability, why spend the summer at home?

"Um . . . it's mostly because my family's different. We don't go on holiday much except my uncle and me. But I usually take care of my mother cus father has a lot of work to do during this time," Loukas tried to explain. "I help her around. She can get pretty snappy, but she's a lovely lady."

Loukas smiled and laughed at the memories. "Sometimes she jokes about how I don't have a brain and my uncle used to say I should think more, so I get them being a little stressed around me. My uncle was very close with her when they were kids, so I understand he wants to make sure she's dealing alright." Loukas sadly looked down into his glass. "Those were the happier times. Nowadays, it's harder, but I have done my best to be a dutiful son but . . ." He didn't want to continue that thought. Instead, he shifted the topic to something more positive. "When she's sad, I will be there. When she's happy,

I will be there. If she ever needs someone to cry on, that will be me. I don't want my little brother to deal with that. I have years of experience and that's how we deal with tough times."

Hide's gaze was on the fishes. Loukas was about to groan about him being distracted, but then he said, "Loulou . . . that's not normal."

"Huh?"

Hide scrunched his nose. "Like a kid should not be his parent's therapist."

"Excuse me?"

"How long was this going on for? This shit's kinda creepy."

"What do you know?" Loukas snapped back. He paused and looked away. "Sorry."

"Well, I guess I don't know Jack," Hide grumbled. "You heard of Oedipus?"

"Hide, it's not like that . . ."

"Oh yeah, maybe her pussy ain't to your liking," Hide said, rolling his eyes.

"Don't talk about my mother like that," Loukas emphasised, every syllable cutting his tongue.

"Christ, Loulou, I'm saying I don't think parents act like this with their kids. It's creepy."

"You wouldn't know the first thing about decent parental relationships or responsibilities, anyway." Loukas immediately regretted what he said as Hide's ears laid flat, his mouth agape. "Hide, I'm—"

The man tugged Loukas down by the necklace and glared at him directly in the eye. "Listen, boy. I know a lot of crap. A lot more crap than you think. If we wanna compare hell, I can give it in great detail."

Loukas tried to tug away, but Hide's grip was firm. The silver of his chain dug into his neck, and he could not look elsewhere; all he could do was stare directly into Hide's eyes with no escape.

"I'm s-sorry . . ."

"I know you are always sorry, so cut that crap out. Let me put it nicely. You don't deserve that shit they throw at you. No kid does. So take that shit and shove it. You got that?"

He was harsh, but his scolding was out of concern. Hide was concerned and lecturing.

CHAPTER 8

So uncomfortable.

"Y-yes sir..."

"Sir?" Hide cocked his head.

"I-I mean Hide. I'm...I...can use the bathroom for a bit."

Hide rolled his eyes. "Fine, you could have gone earlier, but if you wanna cry about it, be my guest. Don't care. Also, don't call me sir. I ain't a sir."

Loukas nodded and rushed to the private restroom, closing the door behind him. He stood at the sink, hugging himself tightly, happy that no one was around to see him like this. In the quiet, his thoughts worsened.

Hide was cute in his clothes, looking so pissed off at me.

Loukas sank to the floor, back pressed against the door. His heart pounded in his chest and he heard his blood rush in his ears. All he could feel then was the bile flowing through his veins, doing nothing for the obvious bulge in his pants that had not calmed down. Especially when Hide yanked his necklace and chastised about how horrible he had been. The feeling of silver moulding into his skin had sent a strange pleasure.

This was not supposed to happen.

The tendrils from his back slipped under his necklace. They were so much harder to control now. Even mild excitement was enough for them to come out. As if to taunt him about how much he wanted to fully give in to his lust. Even if it risked the one friendship that he could not ruin.

Loukas felt his necklace where Hide touched. So safe. As if he belonged to someone. Someone who cared about him. Or used to.

His mother was the one who used to own this piece of jewellery and gave it to him as her gift. His uncle adjusted it just for him. If only it was Hide who cared as much to touch him like that. Only his uncle did, but it certainly never had that love or tenderness.

Maybe Hide would give him a delicate necklace himself someday.

Loukas shook his head at the notion. Hide was a pervert, so maybe he would default to a collar.

Tight with dark black leather.

His rough callus hands around his neck, pressing against the buckle.

It would be so nice to be under Hide's care like that, where he would be loved as a sweet pet. The older man's firm guiding hands caressing Loukas' face after claiming him as his new puppy.

Loukas let out a moan when the tendrils slipped into his jeans. They dripped with slippery, milky fluid as they wrapped around his hardening cock. A part of him wanted to be mortified at what was happening, but he did not care. It felt so good and Hide was too perfect for this. He was so stern, stubborn, and irresistible.

The tendril, aided by its slick, stroked his shaft. Loukas raised his hands to his mouth, biting his hand, holding back the noises within his throat as he pressed his back to the door.

Hide did not know how strongly his presence made him feel. The goat's body pressed against his and the pungent odour oozing from the man's every pore was aggravating. Loukas had touched himself many times, remembering the scars he had left on Hide's body.

Loukas could imagine how it looked now. Hide's shoulder, torn as he bled on the bed. Maybe Loukas had been a terrible dog with him and could not help but bite his master. Hide would need to tug on Loukas' leash so he would behave better.

That image in his mind was not enough.

The real Hide would run away if he tried such aggression and devotion. What if Loukas cut his ankles and watched him crawl around in agony? He might get used to it.

Because Hide was his and vice versa.

Hide would learn to understand his horrible love. He would enjoy the twisted repulsive thing Loukas had for him. A desire that made him only want to break the other man, be owned by him, and eat him all at once.

Hide's body was perfect. His tears were delicious, and his insides were his true beauty.

Loukas was panting. His hips kept jerking into the tentacles. Those extra appendages tugged his chain, massaging the tender skin underneath. The others pumped his cock faster as Loukas' mind went further into his fantasy.

He—

"Loulou?"

CHAPTER 8

Time stopped at that one word.

Hide stood behind him, and the door opened.

His ears were flat against his head, his shoulder strap hanging off his shoulder.

The little goat's face had his mouth and his eyes wide.

"I-I . . ."

Loukas could not bring any words from his brain to his lips. His tendril halted mid-stroke, having no time to feel any sort of relief.

They did the worst thing possible instead.

They reach out aggressively, sending Loukas into a panic.

"No!" he shouted, but it was too late.

The tendrils gripped Hide by his torso and arms and pulled him roughly to Loukas.

Why now?

Loukas did not know what to do, he did not want to hurt him, yet his awful personality still loved how tightly Hide was held. He wanted to see more.

"Whoa! What the hell!" Hide shouted, face to face with Loukas. Their noses bumped into each other, and Loukas could feel his hot breath against his skin. His body pressed against him. It went straight to his stiffening erection.

"I'm so-sorry! Please bite or something, so I c-can let go," Loukas begged.

How could he even explain this?

Any of this.

The tendrils curled around Hide's body, going under his shirt. "Is it just me, or are these things not so rough this time?" Hide's laughter was strained.

His body was motionless, as if cautious about what Loukas was about to do.

"I'm not sure," Loukas stammered. Maybe he was in denial, but the tendrils' grip, although tight, was not as tight as it could have been.

They were aggressive, but the way they squirmed over Hide's body seemed more curious rather than malicious.

"What did I say about apologising so much?" Hide huffed, flaring his nostrils, calming down from the initial fright. "You just got horny, nothing more to it than th—ah!"

Hide was cut off by a tendril sliding into his shorts. His hips lurched forward, and Loukas could see a small bulge underneath his tight shorts.

Such a sensual sight for him. Hide's body caressed and toyed with before his very eyes.

"St-still, I have to stop these th-things," Loukas said, searching around for anything to end all of this.

Hide gave him the unmistakable look of lust in his grey eyes.

"Let's be real. You really wanna get off. And those things seem to like me a bit too much." He allowed a tentacle to wrap around his wrist. "Maybe I can help you out again."

This was not happening

"You're n-not a little afraid?"

His eyes were glued to Hide. This scenario had only ever been realistic in his increasingly frustrating dreams.

Hide gave the appendage a light kiss, winking in Loukas' direction. "If it makes you calm down. This is nothing."

Loukas wanted to reject it. This sort of understanding and acceptance was not normal. Hide was a little crude man, but he was not a freak. He did not deserve to be dragged into any of this. They should not even be doing this.

He should not . . .

His smile was beautiful.

Hide's hands were on Loukas' thigh, grin wide. He licked his lips and said, "I can make it quick, you know. I'm a master of my craft." His hands slowly crept down the ginger's stomach to a bush of pubic hair just an inch away from where he wanted them the most. "Relax, baby boy, let me handle it. We already did a little phone stuff, anyway. I'm glad to see you got a fire crotch to match the drapes."

Hide was exactly where Loukas always wanted him to be.

If Loukas were to have his first time, he wanted it to be with Hide and no one else.

"Okay," was Loukas' reply. He moved a hand over Hide's pretty face and saw his bright missing-tooth smile.

"I've . . . I've never done this before. A-any of this." Loukas knew that

CHAPTER 8

was not something he should be ashamed of, but he could not help but feel embarrassed admitting that to someone like Hide.

The goat was so much more experienced. How could Loukas ever compete or know if he were doing anything right?

"Ah, so big ass virgin? I can't see why though with the two litre soda bottle you're packing," Hide said as he casually swatted tendrils around Loukas' exposed dick and gave a low whistle. "And without the foreskin—rare in these parts. Does it get cold without the peen hood?"

"N-no, I . . ." This was bewildering. Loukas shook his head as he tried to respond. "W-what? I-I just had no one, um, offer. Ah!"

Hide's hand cradled his dick, moving his hand slowly up and down the shaft, causing Loukas to let out a series of uninhibited moans.

This was beyond what he imagined. Hide's warm, perfect hand, the texture of his palm, how agonisingly slow and terrific his thumb felt on the underside of the head.

More, please, more.

"Now, is this better than your hands you have been using these past few months?" Hide teased, fondling the slit.

"Y-yes, it's s-so much better. D-don't st-stop," Loukas blurted out.

"Too much already? Shame, you're a fast shooter. Poor thing. Can you hold back a little, baby boy? Just for me, your good sir?"

"Yes, I c-can, sir. I can."

He normally would have hated how desperate he sounded. Like a lascivious fool. But this was beyond his dreams and fantasies.

He heard Hide's groans and felt the goat rocking against his thigh. His hard hot fat penis pressed against him underneath layers of cloth.

Then Loukas finally knew what was happening. Those tendrils had long since left him alone and were left to their genuine desire.

They had pulled down the goat's shorts and underwear and wrapped themselves around his chubby cock. Its shiny head poked out of the scrunchy layer of foreskin just for Loukas to see. In that beautiful voice Hide whispered, "Good boy," as he bent down. Loukas internally prayed to not finish right there and then from mere touch alone.

The older man's soft, perfect lips gave a ghost of a kiss on the head of Loukas' dick, giving Loukas a good preview of what was to come.

Hide opened his mouth and licked the wide head before he suckled the very tip. His lips went straight to work, his mouth was so skilled. The suction was as if it was made specifically for him. Loukas wondered why he did not blow at that exact moment from how it overwhelmed his mind with an undiluted carnal desire.

He agreed to be good and not cum so fast. He would be good.

I would be a good boy to my da—Hide.

The tendrils jerked Hide's cute pocket-size dick as he moaned over Loukas' shaft. In response, the man's fingers wrapped themselves around Loukas' cock and inch by inch, it entered his mouth.

Hide's tongue was sublime as it laid flat, caressing the thick shaft down to the base, brushing against his pubic hair. Loukas' panting quaked the more he slid into the wet heat. Hide could not take his entire thing, right?

He simply couldn't.

As if to prove him wrong, Hide's throat enclosed Loukas' member until there was nothing left for the beast-kin's hands to grip, freeing them to cradle Loukas' heavy balls. His nose nuzzled into his pubic hair, his heavy breaths rustling the coarse strands.

To further the audacity of it all, in a silent "I win," Hide looked him directly in the eyes.

"Fuck," Loukas allowed from his lips.

Distantly, he reprimanded himself for such foul language. But he did not care. He could hear Hide inhale sharply as the tendrils pumped his little cock even faster. One wrapped around the goat's thigh, moving to his ass just beneath his tail.

Loukas' desire by proxy pressed itself against Hide's hole, rubbing it with slick. Hide shuddered as it slowly prodded him open.

Loukas should have been inside of him instead of the tentacle. It should be him fucking Hide. Filling that body with his love.

The tendrils moved even faster.

Loukas grabbed Hide by the horns. He heard Hide make a strangled noise

CHAPTER 8

as Loukas glided his mouth back and forth over his cock.

Hide, sweet Hide.

He wanted to destroy that perfect body and open it up.

Loukas saw tears leak from the corner of the man's eyes and his hand tapping at his abdomen. The tendril fucked Hide even rougher.

Was it too much?

Those tears are perfect. Please cry more for me.

It was only a bigger turn-on.

Why was Loukas so ashamed? He crossed so many lines before, so why not another?

If it felt good to give in, why not give in all the way?

He wanted to . . .

He needed to . . .

"H-hide," Loukas moaned as he burst into the goat's mouth.

He felt the entire world slow to a crawl, pumping his hips into that mouth over and over to fill Hide's belly with every drop of his built-up frustration. His grasp was rough, and he imagined tearing those horns straight from the skull.

It was so delicious.

Loukas gasped for breath as he came down from his high. His gaze fell on Hide-in-reality and got a good look at him.

The man's mouth filled with his seed. Some fluid spurted out of Hide's nose as he struggled for air.

His chubby cock still stood firm.

"*Hack.* Fuck, Loulou, ha, ha. You . . .," Hide coughed, holding his neck.

He was . . .

Loukas pulled him into a kiss, wrapping his hand around Hide's wide dick and roughly stroking it. Hide squealed in his mouth and Loukas hoped it was from the overwhelming bliss of his kiss and his hand. It was him that was making Hide feel good and no one else should ever get this privilege.

Loukas had seen how Hide stroked him, so he might as well return the favour.

If Hide were to climax, it would be from his own hand.

Loukas' growing tongue swirled in his mouth, allowing it to slip down Hide's throat. He savoured the salty, bitter fluids that once filled it. All to clean every drop possible.

Hide rocked into Loukas' fist, as clumsy as it was. Occasionally he held too loose, making Hide rock even faster. Sometimes too tight and Hide groaned, hitting Loukas on his back to slow down.

His moans grew in pitch until Loukas felt sticky cum coat his palm and his shirt. The kiss broke and Loukas finally eyed Hide and couldn't help but feel more infatuated. He enjoyed Hide's bruised red lips, cut by his sharp teeth. Blood flowed down his chin. He was sweaty and his hair stuck to his forehead. His face was flushed and his eyes were wet.

He was so beautiful. Loukas just had to lap at the tears running down Hide's face and the milky residue from his nose.

Loukas' gaze landed on his hand, covered in Hide's spunk. His musk was all him on and was heaven itself. Loukas slathered his tongue over his fingers, cleaning it up in front of the goat. He wanted him to watch and see how much he would do.

"Shit, you're . . . aggressive with this." Hide wiped his lips as he tried to catch his breath.

Loukas observed the man again as he tried licked away the dribble of blood from his busted lip..

"Hmm."

"You're so damn rough it's ridiculous." Hide's ears were flat like the tone of his voice, and it put Loukas on edge. Was Hide upset with him? "You're lucky my gag reflex is practically non-existent."

"Thank you . . ."

"I . . ." Hide paused before letting out a sigh. His brows knitted as if contemplating something. "Yeah, I guess that you're welcome."

Wait . . .

Was he too rough?

Did they just . . .

The high had ended, and they left as two sober men staring at each other, realising what thin line they had crossed.

CHAPTER 8

"I . . . Wow it's—fuck." Hide scratched the back of his ear. Loukas tried to open his mouth to say something, but all that came out was nothing.

"Crap, it's late, you know, haha," Hide laughed as Loukas got off the floor.

"Yeah . . ."

Hide dusted himself off, going to the sink to swish water in his mouth. "So you've never done this before, period? Guy or otherwise, right? I'll probably let you off easier if that's the case."

"No . . ." Loukas prodded at the ground, unable to get the one phrase out of his mind.

I was too rough and kissed Hide.

"This is . . . my first time."

"I could tell. I guess having a decent first time is better than having a crappy one." Hide picked up his phone and turned to Loukas, grinning. Something about it seemed too forced. "Anyway, I'm glad you had a good time today. Happy twenty-first birthday. I have things to do and a ride to get to in a few minutes."

Loukas pulled out of his stupor too late as Hide was already out of the bathroom and running out of the pod.

Filled with regret, Loukas chased after him. As fast as Hide was, Loukas was too determined to let that stop him. He finally caught up and held Hide by the shoulders.

"Hey! What the hell!"

"I'm sorry I kissed you."

Hide rolled his eyes. "Seriously, is that . . .fuck, it's just your first man kiss. It's nothing. You'll get a better one from a guy your age, anyway."

Hide really didn't get it.

"I . . . I'm s-sorry if I was too . . . rough."

Hide raised a brow at him and said, "Of course it's you of all people who would apologise for that."

"Huh, what d-do you mean?"

"Oh, nothing, just doing some thinking." Hide seemed to look past him rather than at him. "Anything else you want? Other than standing there."

"I . . . I like it. T-to kiss. I want to kiss you again."

Hide stared at him. "What? Why?"

Because I like you.

"Just . . . again." Loukas has never been more desperate than he was at that moment.

"I'm . . . I'm not the kind of guy you should have your first time with, alright?" Hide looked away. "Like you probably can get someone more—"

"I don't mind if it's you . . . I liked that it was you." Loukas said. "Someone I know. My best friend." Loukas' heart was beating so fast.

Hide was weighing something in his mind before he sighed and said, "I mean, it's a kiss, and not even your first actual kiss. It may not mean that much, anyway."

"I . . . I still don't mind that." Stooping to the other man's level with shaky hands, he asked, "C-can I kiss you, Hide . . . Is that okay?"

"Yes, yes, I'm standing out here sweating in the sun. Just do it," Hide snorted.

With shaky hands, their lips met briefly.

Unlike the frenzied heat of the moment from before, Loukas relished just how soft Hide's lips were, how his calloused hands held his face so gently.

It ended with Hide pulling away again, hand on mouth as before. His expression was unreadable.

"Th-thank you. Um, I had a good time," Loukas said

"Yeah, I could tell." Hide was glaring at him.

Did he do something wrong?

Hide's ears perked up at the sound of something and he waved Loukas off. "But my ride's here. See you around, Loulou. It's late as hell. Hope you get a lot more love when school starts. Your dick could go places, hehe."

And with that, Hide sped off while Loukas stood behind him.

He could not leave him alone like that. Not after what happened. Loukas was not sure why, but Hide seemed upset. Not able to let go, Loukas followed him as quietly as he could this time.

A growing sense of regret filled him.

Why did he ask for more?

The man was already uncomfortable, yet Loukas just did not know to take the hint.

CHAPTER 8

(He probably only allowed you to use his mouth out of pity, and you took it too far. Why else would he be so cautious? You saw how he is with other men, allowing them to do whatever they want. You're no better.)

He finally caught up to the man and saw exactly who his ride was. Hide hugged that familiar brown fox, face in his chest, hands clutching his shirt.

(You upset him. Congratulations, you fucked up again.)

Makhi patted Hide's back. Loukas did not care how deep he was biting into his hands watching this.

"Something wrong?" the fox asked.

"I'll talk about it later . . ."

The fox laughed brightly, and it made Loukas sick.

"Alright, maybe we can play some Star Battle later tonight and you'll feel better, okay?"

Loukas could not watch it any more. He took it too far. At the end of the day, Hide always would have that fox. Hide was Loukas' first, but Loukas would never be his first in anything.

There the man stood watching on and learning his place in Hide's life. As a simple blot and maybe even as one of the many other people who hurt him.

Out of sight, away from the crowd, Loukas could not stop screaming.

CHAPTER 9

No calls, no follow-up.

Just when Loukas thought everything was getting better, he had to crash back down to reality. This time, that crash tinted his loneliness with hatred.

Loukas could taste the goat on his lips even though a week had passed. The salty taste of his seed he had fed the man was still ever so bitter. When he closed his eyes, he saw Hide's breathless, flushed face and bruised lips. It all slipped away in one day—like that, Hide ran back to Makhi, into his arms.

Loukas never hated anyone more than that fox. He was not that naïve; he knew what kinds of things Hide did for his *friends*. His close friends who would warm his bedside and fuck him into the ground.

What a horrible, wretched creature Hide was with.

"Puppy? Are you okay?" Xander entered his room. He frowned at the sight of Loukas, who had not left his bed in days.

"No . . . I'm not," Loukas murmured. How could he be fine?

He had his first time and had nothing to show for it. It was meaningless to everyone else but him.

"Well, you can tell me. Last week, you were so excited about going out to that fair. If only I was not busy, I would have taken you much earlier. I thought today would be perfect given it's your special," The other man laughed. "But when I got back, you did not want to leave any more."

Special day? He hasn't felt it was anything worth thinking about in years.

CHAPTER 9

Loukas wondered how much he should tell, but it was already too late to hide anything. So he said, "I went with Hide . . . W-we . . . we did some things afterwards and I-I kissed him and it scared him."

Loukas clutched the pillow to his face. "I . . . I fucked up."

Xander was quiet for a while after that. It was to the point that Loukas worried that Xander had left him, until he heard a sigh.

"It's okay when that happens. It's just an uncontrollable outcome." Xander rubbed Loukas' back to soothe him.

But Loukas did not feel one bit relaxed. Bitterness filled his mind and body and all he wanted was to scream.

"It's not okay!" Loukas snapped.

"How about this?" Xander's eyes narrowed. "I know Hide, and the one thing he hates more than commitment is devotion like yours."

His tone was harsh and to the point, as if to emphasise that he screwed up and there was nothing he could do about it.. Loukas could not even hate himself more than now. He was such a fool.

"B-But he never . . . He hugged his best friend. Th-they're affectionate."

"Hm? Ah! He's got another boy around." Xander seemed amused. "Typical. Hide has a type, as you can tell."

Freckles on Makhi's face, two sharp fangs in his mouth . . .

"Has he ever introduced you to any of his friends? Since he was so happy to introduce you to his *special* friend."

Loukas paused as his mind went back to the only friend Hide introduced him to. A surly fox beast-kin named Makhi, whose arms he would run into and hold tight. The goat's lips said "friend," but how he held the other man's body was intimate, how his face lit up whenever he was around was angelic. That was the "friend" Hide wanted him to meet.

No one else.

Hide had a whole life, and it was clear he did not consider Loukas a part of it. Not a respectable part of it, anyway.

Xander raised a brow and said, "Your hands are bleeding."

Loukas looked down and saw how clenched his fists were. His nails dug into his skin, drawing blood. But he could not bring himself to care about it.

"N-no, just Makhi. He's with him."

Xander rubbed his back again. "You already know what that means, boy. He did the same with me. It was not pleasant."

That fox, that man that Hide liked so much. A man he called a friend, but Loukas knew Hide well enough. Makhi was a friend who had his dirty claws all over him, and tasted places Loukas could only dream of.

Why him?

Hide has a type.

Freckles, sharp teeth.

Maybe I can make Hide see how much I want him. That fox would be better off dead and then I would be the only one in his life, right?

If there were anyone else, then I could deal with every single one of them. So I would be his one and only.

"So, my most precious Puppy," Xander whispered into his rage-blinded ear. The blond's hands were over Loukas' chest, some rubbing the fabric of his shirt against his skin. "I got a little present for you and I promise it will make it all better."

"What?" Loukas was breathing too fast. "What will make it all better? Hide picked a fox over me. He chose him over me every time. All because, unlike him, he's not rotten."

"I know, but I feel it may help you understand a few things. Just remember, I would never leave you, okay?"

The man removed a lock of Loukas' hair from his eyes. He was so gentle that Loukas just wanted to hold him and bawl.

The boy sniffled, wanting to tear off his skin. This time, however, unlike anyone else, Xander accepted what he was.

"Okay . . . you can show me," Loukas whispered. He had a feeling what this was, but instead of apprehension, he just felt comfort.

"Perfect," Xander said, holding the boy close to his body. Safe and exactly where he belonged.

* * *

CHAPTER 9

The sun was barely hovering over the horizon, ready to dip below and bring everything into the night. To obscure any potential eyes from what depravities that might occur once all closed their eyes.

That was what Loukas thought as they were at the warehouse again, climbing down those steps. His stomach clenched in discomfort at where he was and what had transpired there before. Debauchery, blood, and other such vile things. But he was not good enough to turn back or refuse.

"Um, Xander I'm not sure—"

"Hush, Pet, it's okay." Xander's hand clenched his palm so tightly that Loukas worried the man would break something. However, his firm and powerful grip brought Loukas relief. As if it was the one thing tethering him to reality.

Down those steps, and through the door, Loukas saw what Xander was dying to show him.

Huddled in the middle of the room were several men tied up individually by rope. The cloth in their mouths muffled their cries.

Most of them were beast-kin: a deer, cat, rabbit, and rat. Some were much older men, even older than Xander. All were terrified of the pair as they entered the room.

"What are you doing?" Loukas asked, but he deep down knew what this was. He felt a pair of arms around his waist. A hand cupped his face.

"I know what you did to my neighbour last year. He went over to you and now it's been months and I have not seen him since." Xander's breath was in his ear. "Do you know who he is? A big powerful man, a tad on the shabby side."

That description was so much like the man Loukas killed and ate in front of Hide. The first person he killed had known Xander.

Xander continued and said, "He mostly helped me with my groceries, a usual drifter of the area, but now he's gone. A decent man when he was off work and had a girlfriend at home, so I heard."

Guilt filled his stomach, and Loukas wanted to die.

"'I'm—I'm s—sorry, so v—very sorry.' Is that what you want to say?" Xander whispered into his ear, playfully mocking his stutter, reminding Loukas how pitiful he sounded to every other normal person in his life. "Despite what you say, you still can't help indulging again."

He was sorry.

Loukas felt his chest tighten as it burned from the inside.

"I . . . I know . . . I . . . Can we talk about something else? I don't want to," Loukas said, averting his eyes from the other demon's unwavering gaze.

"Why don't you just eat? You're starving yourself on purpose. You killed once you got hungry enough, right? That's why you worry me. You simply are a danger to yourself."

Xander's golden eyes shone with pity, and it made Loukas sick. He did not deserve this. No apologies could change what he had done and what he was about to do.

He wanted to tell Xander that his touches were uncomfortable.

But why?

No one else would even breathe the same air as him if they knew what Xander knew.

"I can't. I never wanted to eat anything."

Xander knew the full extent of Loukas' hunger, but the fact he still was touching his body was a testament to his care. Or that's what Loukas told himself.

"You say you don't want to, but if I leave this room with you alone with them, would you still kill and eat them?"

Loukas wiped away his tears with the back of his hand as Xander spoke. He would not resist. He could try to even run away, but someone would get hurt. Someone always got hurt.

"You can't deny it, can you? You're a special boy. That's why I want you to eat."

Xander's unnerving statement sounded more like an order when he said it. His now green eyes almost shimmered in the dim light. They were like the foliage that surrounded the lakes of Loukas' scattered memories with his uncle. A forest even the most seasoned traveller could get lost in.

The difference was it never changed. It never became blood-red, nor filled him with such a paralysing sense of dread.

CHAPTER 9

Even now Loukas could remember that lake.

"It wasn't always l-like this. I-I was . . . was normal." Loukas didn't know what he was saying, but it was getting harder to focus. The tied-up witnesses were growing more frantic in their struggle to break free. But it was no use.

There was only one exit, and Loukas, who wanted the roaring in his head to stop, blocked it.

Something seemed strange.

"There, there, Pet, let it all out," said a voice Loukas vaguely heard as he sank further into his mind.

Shouting, pain, and growing fear tainted Loukas' old memories. The only difference between now and back then was that he was stronger as a child. He could have bore it all with a smile on his face. Now he was just a monster that had replaced their prized son and still had the audacity to use his name.

He had his difficulties and his fears, but at least his parents loved him back then. They had to, right?

They should have loved him, because if they never . . .

What was the point?

The memories whirled and crashed within him. He had died and had been gutted by sharp metal.

Mother . . .

After that day, her nails clung to him and never let go. Many saw it as cowardly every time he reacted with fear. He remembered how brave he used to be. Every time he flinched, many would remind him of how affectionate he used to be.

Every time he wanted to die, she wished he did so. There were days he wondered if others were right. Maybe he shouldn't have woken up that day.

"Puppy, you should be happy you're here." Xander held his face so gently, and his other hand undid the top button of his shirt. "Because there's nothing you"— his hands slipped under Loukas' shirt and caressed his shoulders and the dip of his clavicle—"can do about it. I'm happy you are here as you are."

Loukas felt his heart flutter from the remark. No one had ever said that to him. He did not understand why anyone would want him around. The closest was Hide, but the goat was much better off without him.

Loukas' head felt fuzzy and hot, and the touches fanned his arousal. The skin of the man before him looked more and more desirable.

"Thank you," he said.

Xander nuzzled into his neck. "Let me help you. You can't help yourself, so let me handle everything. As a pet is nothing without his master."

Loukas gazed at that smile so desperate to help him. No matter what Hide said, Xander cared. He truly cared about him.

The man's lip met his.

It surprised Loukas, and he did not know how to react. It was unlike anyone he had ever kissed before. The time he kissed Hide was so sickly magical, it was a miracle he had not done worse.

This time, he did not know what to think or even do.

It tasted of bitter roots and citrus seeds. Loukas felt sick. The taste turned to one of rotten ash and cement.

Just before he could shove Xander away, he tasted a bloody piece of sweetness leak into his mouth and down his throat like searing coals

Was that meat?

Human flesh . . .

And it was heavenly sweet.

A long tongue ran over his mouth, writhing and thrashing around his own. He distinctly heard a moan as his body was driven to wanton need.

Was it him who moaned?

It was too much.

Loukas' teeth pierced into the tongue squirming in his mouth, tearing the very tip of it out of Xander's maw. Chewy, tough, and tasted of rancid pork—a true demon's torn tongue he'd spat out. The blond demon with blood running down his chin gripped the back of Loukas' orange locks and pulled him deeper into the kiss. Loukas chewed that now-stump, not for a meal, but out of instinct. He chewed to taste what felt so familiar. It was so much like him.

Rotting from the inside.

The world felt so fuzzy . . .

He smelled sweet fear in the room as their guests watched on.

CHAPTER 9

Loukas would be an obedient puppy for Xander.

Screams filled Loukas' ears, and he savoured the taste of delicious flesh in his mouth. Chewing it like gum, then spitting out.

He enjoyed the feeling of being able to indulge in the forbidden pleasures that he denied from himself for so long.

He gutted the men one by one with a knife, pulling out their bags of digestive fluids. It was nostalgic in a way. As a much younger boy, he used to help his uncle clean the deer he caught on those peaceful autumn days. The man considered it a treat to let his nephew shoot and clean his own game. He used to hate how those poor animals eyes were filled with fear as they bled out. However, to impress the one family member who had not given up on him yet, Loukas simply did as was expected and felt so loved in return. That was the one gift he wouldn't trade anything for in the world. Now those same fear-ridden eyes of these men were a turn on, and he needed more of this intoxicating terror.

One man, braver than the rest, somehow managed to get his legs free and began to kick Loukas away in a vain attempt to escape. Now, that energy was exactly what Loukas wanted. With little effort, the brave soul was soon screaming as Loukas pinned him to the ground and sliced a small cut into his abdomen. With this much energy he could last longer during things like this.

The screams grew louder as Loukas shoved his hands into the slit-like opening searching around in the warm and moist cave. If only there was a way to make people stay alive and aware for longer during things like this. Alas, he could only do so much before their bodies gave out. He wasted no time finding the small intestines and as carefully as he could, slowly pulled them from his newly made opening. It was like dragging a very long worm from its burrow accompanied by hellish wails that were made for a demon like himself.

Loukas resisted his urge to kiss him for making such music to his ears. His lips were for Hide, not for any other man after all. Loukas was interrupted when he found the long tube of flesh growing taut. It was stuck or he had reached the end of this meat rope. The screams had been reduced to soft sobs as Loukas tried to tug a little harder to continue his entertainment.

With greater use of his strength, Loukas did not hold back as he yanked the intestinal rope, tearing it off of something from within. To his delight, he was rewarded with more screams that gradually became silent as the last bit of intestine was removed.

Loukas stood over the body, slurping up his hard-earned meal that he had just torn out. He heard the screams of "monster" and "demon" hurled at him from the spectators as he finished the delicious innards in one final gulp. They could all keep calling him that; he had the whole day to bring out much worse names from those beautiful mouths.

Unlike his previous attempts at flaying, Loukas wondered whether keeping someone upside down would allowed them to be awake and aware for much longer. Long enough to carefully peel off their skin starting at the feet. One needed a steady hand and a lot of patience to skin deer and not damage the hide, and for a human that was a new level of difficulty that Loukas was prepared to take on.

The gift of even a peek of those divine muscles and pulsing blood vessels in their natural state made his cock jump. For once, he stopped worrying about going too far and simply enjoyed how rich the men smelled to him. He soon stood before the twitching anatomical model dangling upside down with rope, with its mouth fixed in a permanent scream. In his scarred hands was the flawless skin of a racoon beast-kin. He messed up when he got to the tail, losing the part he wanted to keep the most.

His sight locked on the remaining victims, whose curses and names had since stopped. Those who still had the will to escape were outright thrashing against their binds, willing to even break their own limbs for freedom. The others were either crying or sat frozen, staring at the now-skinless and wheezing remnants of a person, maybe even aware how little control everyone in this room had over things.

A wisp of melancholy came to Loukas at that thought. He was sorry for not drowning as he should have all those many years ago. It was what the Lord and his parents intended, but he was too stubborn to allow that. Now he was a thing that took on that dead boy's life. However, he felt little guilt or remorse towards his enjoyment towards having many more tries at skinning.

CHAPTER 9

Loukas was not sorry for liking what he liked, his true self.

The wails that came from his next skinning attempt affirmed his convictions. From the drops of sweat that dripped from their pores to the occasional subtle twitch of a muscle, it was an art that made his heart sing. Every one of Loukas' senses wanted him to experience every second of this atrocity committed by his own hands..

And is that so wrong? Why should he be so upset about just relishing something that has only given him love in return?

Loukas couldn't help but notice how suddenly easier it was to lift one of the heavier men. The young man smiled when those slimy tendrils released from his back and another delicious idea popped into his head. He needed the extra help after all, and five hands were always better than two. The pleas for death were cheers of encouragement as he accomplished his goal.

With a sigh of content, Loukas stood by and admired the animalistic shrieking of the now-skinless creature he had come to love. Each of his appendages held a blood-soaked tool for his craft. Scalpels, knives, hammers, and ice picks were now in his grasps and he couldn't wait to make use of them. For once, Loukas was excited to make use of his abnormalities. Why did he dislike them, anyway? They were made for him.

Loukas admired and ran his fingers over his fully intact skin suit. He had to be careful in handling such a thing; his nails could ruin his hard work. Were they always this sharp? That concern vanished when he found that the cute stubby tail remained attached and unharmed. The soft curly fur reminded him of a certain someone. Someone who would rightfully hate him if he used the skin to make a doll in their likeness. A small goat beast-kin doll to dress up and give his full love to since he couldn't give it to the real version.

No one could love a thing like himself, a monster. However, if he couldn't get that kind of love, then he could get the next best thing. He didn't want to be looked upon as a mentally stunted child or a pathetic waste of space. Loukas' desire was for his victim's final thoughts to be of him and only him as the only thing that mattered. Until they drew their final breath.

So he decided to feast.

With a power drill, he bore a nice hole into the back of a bald skull. In and out the metallic bit went, shredding the thick bone underneath all while the skull's owner begged for mercy. How wonderful it was to see such a smart, distinguished man become only capable of incomprehensible noises as the drill hit the soft brain tissue. Blood flowed from his nose and the now-brain dead man voided his bowels.

It was too much to bear, so Loukas got on all fours and pounced on the body, his claw tearing into the skin, eliciting pitiful cries. Loukas was panting as he savoured the intoxicating fear.

This hole was too small to fit him, Loukas thought, licking at his jagged claws. Plus, he did want to be so vulgar as to do such a thing without permission first. The other man looked so small underneath him. Just like Hide.

He wanted to . . .

He needed to.

His tendril picked up the hammer and aimed at the top of the skull where he had previously drilled. Loukas watched his toy straight into those confused tearful eyes. It would be alright, he would make a much bigger hole to use when it was all over.

"You're doing such a wonderful job my sweet Puppy." Xander was laughing as he stood by and watched. He smiled at Loukas with pride, something that had not happened in a long time.

Someone was proud of him. He was wanted.

"I know what you want to do, and I think it's a lovely idea. You're the most excellent creature I have ever met." In his hands was a camera aiming its full attention on him. Xander was so kind to him. "Hmm, I wonder if this would count as beast with that kind of body. Oh well, not of my concern. It will attract more niche viewers."

What was he talking about? It probably didn't matter. To Xander, he was perfect. The things he tried to suppress were what made him excellent to a man like him. His true nature, as repugnant as it was to the world, was as natural as breathing, so why should he hide it? He had failed to live as the man everyone wanted, so why not live as the horrible monster he always had been? Xander accepted him as he was.

CHAPTER 9

The hammer came down with a swift, wet smash, shattering bone. Chunks of blood-soaked brain tissue flew in every direction. Some bits splattered the remaining onlookers, re-energizing a few back into screaming.

Loukas tried to stand up and approach his work only to find that too difficult to do. For some reason, walking on his hands and feet felt so much more natural to him. Did he even like walking on two legs?

He observed the cracked open skull and he found it big enough for him to indulge. The spongy tissue within would feel good around his cock. How long would he even last? It would be nice to fill the dead body with his love nectar in private. Maybe he could ask to do this again off camera; he'd have a lot more bodies to try out by then. Loukas, however, would be as gentle as he could. He needed to practise lovemaking so he would be ready to have his first time going all the way with Hide.

Loukas mounted his toy.

"Good boy, show your viewers how my sweet Puppy makes love." Xander's full attention was on him. He was one of the few who saw how rotten Loukas was deep down and still wanted him.

His love, the defilement of the dead, and arousal at others' fears took centre stage in this friendship, but that was still acceptance in Loukas' eyes. For Xander was the only one who loved him despite all that.

"Happy birthday, Puppy," Xander said.

CHAPTER 10

Hide groaned as he got up from the tiled floor and gave one last check-up on the fridge. He was not sure how these crappy things broke down, but one thing he knew was no one else but him would fix it. It took his mind off the things that shouldn't be bothering him in the first place. However, this time, not even the familiar chill of metal at his fingertips could get rid of the annoying voices in his head.

Well, Loukas likes me.

I was Loukas' first kiss, and the boy wanted more. Not too surprising. I'm good with my mouth.

Really was Loukas' first everything.

The blow job was something he could brush off with ease, but he could not get the taste of Loukas' salty lips out of his head. Nor Loukas' sharp teeth that left cuts over his mouth.

A silly virgin boy with devotion deep as the ocean had kissed him and begged him to stay for another.

Ever since then, Hide had not bothered to call him back, especially when he remembered how thoughtless Loukas was when he sucked him off. Or at least that was what Hide wanted to hold on to as a reason to ghost. Regardless, every time Hide thought about reaching out, he always found another excuse not to do it. Even though Loukas was staying with that horrible man, Hide kept his distance.

CHAPTER 10

The goat ran his tongue over his lips the healing sores left. Why did the kiss bother him more than Loukas' roughness? Hide had done this many times before and would give thousands more kisses afterwards.

Maybe the biggest difference was that he enjoyed it.

"You don't look too good," Makhi said with a wince. He wrung a wet towel and handed it to Hide.

Hide snatched it, hopped over to the sofa, and flopped it over his forehead.

"Excuse me for the evil sun god wanting to kill me," Hide grumbled. He lazily sighed into the cool dampness of the fabric.

Fevers, infection, and probably now has heat fatigue all within the last few weeks were a sign that something had cursed him. He always had poor health, but this past year had been pushing things.

What was next, pneumonia?

Leprosy?

Makhi noted Hide's exhaustion and took out a pair of magazines to fan him.

"I'm just glad you got out of there. I was kinda worried when you said you needed to be picked up and were with that guy. Didn't he kiss you out of nowhere? I can't imagine what would happen if you hadn't left." Makhi gave him a light nudge on the shoulder in the hope of some humour out of all this. It wasn't much, but Hide still took the concern like a man dying of thirst.

For the past few days, the fox insisted Hide stay at his place for a while. The main reason was that he was worried Loukas might do something drastic, especially with Hide not responding to him afterwards..

Hide knew if he told Makhi that Loukas had already followed them before, he might panic and try to get out of town. He didn't want to stress the fox out with an obsessive guy taking their interactions the wrong way; it was not exactly a pleasant thing to have on your mind. There was also his slightly selfish reason. If Makhi left, Hide wouldn't be able to follow. He could come and go as he pleased while he, even after all these years, was never allowed to follow.

Not that Hide blamed Makhi for panicking, he just doubted Loukas would do anything. Damn, he really must have softened his paranoia.

He had kept his ears on alert for years every second he was awake. So, of course, he would notice Loukas was following them. He heard the boy's footsteps and caught a fast glimpse of orange as he hugged Makhi.

He was not sure how to feel as his hive of thoughts swarmed within him, not one of them making sense.

"It's whatever, not the first guy who wants a little kiss. Thanks for your cool ride back there," Hide laughed.

"No problem," Makhi said, taking his seat. In his hands was a console controller, offering it to Hide. "One round? While you get better?"

Hide glanced at the controller and said, "Sure, I got all day, anyway. Any where's better than the sun outside."

He snatched the controller from Makhi, and the fox switched on the box, ready to start a match. "Still, I'm kinda surprised a young guy is that interested in you. Especially a freshman college kid," he said.

"He'll get over it."

Hide needed to stop thinking so hard. He did not want to look into what happened. Loukas kissed him. A boy barely old enough to enter a strip club kissed him.

Loukas' grip was so strong and rough.

"Hey, maybe you can get a driver's licence some time." Makhi, of course, wanted to lighten the mood.

"Nope, ain't interested in getting some government tracking on me." Hide scoffed at the concept, regardless. His reason generally got certain people off his back about that so he was gonna stick with it.

The match started, and he could not concentrate. His attention was all on the fox. Makhi's cheery, smiling face and sharp canines and his lightly scattered freckles.

"Seriously? What's the worst that could happen?" Makhi was kicking his ass.

Hide's palms sweated.

"Well, Fluffy Tail, you just put yourself in their registration willingly. I'm no sucker, unlike everyone else. I know you can't trust those government losers."

CHAPTER 10

It could not stay like this.

"You know, what if I say once you get a licence you could get like a big truck and—?"

Hide's lips met the fox's.

Something he wanted to do for so long.

His tongue was in his mouth, and Makhi's eyes widened at the desperate embrace.

The controller was on the ground, surrounded by empty soda bottles and unwashed clothes.

The game on screen was still ongoing, declaring the obvious winner of the match while their life was on pause.

Eventually, Hide broke free. Makhi's wide green eyes stared back at him and his lips looked so much like they did ten years ago.

Desperate, lonely, intoxicated on booze and dust.

"Makhi, I like you a lot," Hide whispered in his large fluffy ear.

He did it.

He finally said it and . . .

Makhi grabbed his arms, and his smile was strained.

"Hide . . . let's not do that. I . . ."

Something within Hide knew this was not a good sign.

"W-why? Oh, so you can fuck me but not a little kiss," Hide laughed.

What was he doing?

"I mean, yes. I mean, no, but that was you. Fuck." Makhi wiped his lips with the back of his hand. Hide never felt more hurt.

The fox's tail bristled behind him. He continued. "Like you came on to me for that. I just thought of you . . . I just thought you didn't want that kind of stuff."

"What are you talking about?" Hide grit his teeth at what he was hearing.

"Hide, you are just. You always act kinda aggressive every time I used to do something like a hug. So I thought you weren't interested in anything. I don't like you like that, okay?" Makhi lowered his gaze away from him. "I'm sorry for allowing this kind of thing for this long. I just thought you would take the hint. You are my friend, my best friend, but I can't like you like that cus you're just so . . . flakey and I don't get you. Crap, that all sounds bad."

Hint?

The fox seemed so agitated as he took out a cigarette to calm his nerves.

I don't get you.

Those words rang in Hide's mind as he watched the man light up his cigarette.

"I just thought just having sex would be enough. Which was fun and you'd eventually lose interest. Like usual." Makhi looked away from him.

The smoke rose and made Hide's head hurt. Everything was spinning.

"What are you talking about?" Hide growled. His breath was quickening. "I don't want just that."

Hide wondered why he was suffocating suddenly.

Hide just left Alex.

"Then what do you want, Hide? I just don't know what to do with you, okay?" Makhi said, his agitation no longer under layers of false niceties. "Is that what you want to hear?"

Hide was dying.

He had been too stubborn about Carole's house rules and was so damn lonely.

She had not put her foot down with him yet.

As soon as he heard Makhi was coming home honourably discharged, Hide could not stay alone any more.

That desperation Hide had that night filled the hole with empty regret.

Makhi was no longer that plucky girl he had somewhat crushed on. But a stocky man who smiled, and Hide had invited him into Carole's home while he picked up his life.

That night was clear as day. Carole had allowed them to laugh and drink her beer and wine while catching up on old times. Hide got drunk as Makhi was mumbling about leaving.

He grabbed the brown fox's large fluffy tail, clinging to it like a pillow and said, "Don't leave, Fluffy Tail. It's too early. "

"Hide, but it's 10 PM."

"Please, don't leave. You're so cute . . ."

CHAPTER 10

Hide brought the fox's hands up to his throat.
The world was spinning.
"I want you to choke me."

* * *

Hide blinked his eyes to see Makhi's terrified face. The fox held a phone in his ear, chatting with someone.

"I have to squeeze his hand, right? Hide, are you squeezing it?" he said frantically.

Hide looked down and saw his hand held by Makhi's. His chest was on fire and so damn tight he was going to die.

His gaze went to the cigarette that fell from the fox's lips. That awful smoke made his head pound.

"You weren't breathing and I—"

It had been a decade since Hide had a panic attack.

One entire decade where he was fine, yet a single ciggy and some stupid memory were now setting him off.

He should not be this weak.

"Hide?"

Hide shoved his hand away, his teeth bared.

"Stop fucking touching me," Hide snarled, forcing himself to stand, noting how Makhi backed off.

"Shit, you're fine, right?"

No, he was not. He wanted a place to breathe and the fox to tell him everything was okay.

But Makhi would not notice that.

"I'm fine, asshole. I was just trying something cus half my contacts tonight are too busy or too much of my waste of time anyway. Can't believe I was acting like I'm that desperate, gross. " Hide felt sick. The eyes on him drilled into his skin.

Makhi smiled with relief.

He did not notice.

He would never notice.

Hide never told him how much of a fuck-up he was.

And he never would.

"I'm glad, but I'm gladder that you're doing better. You kinda scared me, you know," Makhi said, calming down.

"Yeah, yeah, it's all stupid." Hide hated how he felt like death. "I'm gonna go to Carole's and do some shit. Feeling fucking amazing right now cus now I'm bored with sitting around doing nothing."

The fox looked excited as the whole world felt like static, as Hide gathered his stuff to leave.

"Thank goodness. Um . . . thanks for not taking this the wrong way."

Hide huffed, "Whatever you say. I don't care, anyway."

Hide left through the door and ran.

His stomach hurt, his head hurt, and his chest hurt.

His heart was in pieces.

It all hurt.

CHAPTER 11

Why did he allow these types of things to hurt him? Those memories were all in the past, now they kept coming back, each time just as painful as before.

Few people knew of Hide's life prior, and the ones who did only knew because of his big loud mouth.

Carole was one of those people. She was the one he always went to when he felt his worst. Whenever he needed someone who would stay and somewhat understand. When his mind and body kept being trapped in that house, with the disgusting smoke and greasy hands. She was there, but he could not face her at the moment.

Told you so, she would probably say.

Fuck her.

Loukas . . .

He would not drag that unstable boy into this. He was aware that Alex was probably a worse influence, but as far as Hide knew, he hadn't done anything funny with him yet.

At least that was what he told himself, to ignore the part of him screaming to intervene.

Hide found himself in front of a familiar dingy building. Before him were neon pink lights illuminating the entrance in a dim glow. The pink and blue paint on the building cracked and peeling. Shattered spider webs scored the windows, at least the ones not boarded up.

A tall, bulky, rough-looking man glared at the line of teens with fake IDs, people tweaking with eyes dilated like new moons, and a collection of skimpy men and women trying their luck at a free drink, cash, and bed from someone hopefully horny and not ugly. He was glad he decided on close-toe shoes for tonight with the scattered broken glass bottles and needles all over the disgusting-looking ground. Last thing he wanted was another infection scare.

Hide watched on as thoughts of no longer being sober became more appealing.

Carole could enjoy her drinks, he had to enjoy himself and hopefully be out of his mind for the next several hours. She could take her hypocrisy and shove it. This place, although complete trash, was the best place to find what you were looking for without fear of the police cracking down on you. Toxic Eden, it was called.

Hide made up his mind.

Why should he bother with any of this? Makhi, Loukas, why should he let that shit bother him?

Who cared?

He certainly didn't.

With a false smile and a pair of slightly used pastel sneakers, he gave a wink to the bouncer. "Hey tall and fuckable," he said, leaning against the entrance door.

"Been a while since I've seen yah," the man said as pulled his shades, revealing a pair of slit cat-like eyes looking over the goat with an almost hungry look. Hide tried not to think who it reminded him of and placed a hand on his chest. He wouldn't normally do other beast-kin, but the few who had held his interest had always been carnivorous, with sharp skin-piercing fangs, strong hands, and. . .

Damn it.

"You know I've been a little busy, but right now I'm taking a break. Need a little help getting a drink." Hide licked his lips, pushing away who his thoughts were going to. At least get this cat boy to think he was that horny. It was easier than budgeting the little money he had, anyway.

Which was none.

CHAPTER 11

He observed the man's bushy tail wrapping around Hide's waist.

"Well then, care to tell?"

Hide's hands moved to his groin and lightly pressed against it, gaining the exact reaction he wanted.

"Oh nothing, just some drinks and maybe something nice to lift my mood." He hoped he played his cards right to get at least two free nights.

The cat leaned forward, clearly desiring a little something extra for his help. Hide wanted to gag as he smelt the man's body odour. It was nothing like the now-familiar vanilla of the younger man plaguing his mind. Hide could already tell this would be disappointing by the pathetic size he felt on the man. The only interesting thing was probably the dick being on the more prickly side.

His ears flicked to the sound of a growing irritation and grumbles from the line behind him, cementing his decision to stall. Fuck them, they could wait as he dealt with this guy.

"You are that needy?" The bouncer laughed. "I would love to give a little more right here, but how about a little after work? I'll be free to enjoy that sweet ass for hours. Wouldn't want to hold up this line for too long."

Sure, if Hide was lucky, probably five minutes maximum, but the goat forcefully held his tongue. He did not want to lose money so quickly.

The cat lifted a twenty-dollar bill and Hide resisted the urge to roll his eyes. Cheap ass.

Hide removed his hands and said, "Great idea. We wouldn't want you to get in trouble, right?"

Hide took the bill, glad to avoid a man who had never heard of hygiene in his life. He already fucked this cat before and promised himself to only do that again as a last resort. Even now, he felt sick when he remembered how the blow job he gave became cleaning a thick block of cheese from under the hood of that nasty guy's prickly cock.

The pocket change was pleasant, but Hide was not in the mood to scrub himself for the next three hours. He hoped to find someone else to treat him for the night. Beggars could not be choosers, but he liked his pride.

He gave the beast-kin a wave and made his way inside, hoping he could avoid him for as long as possible. Hide observed the sweaty bodies dancing under the neon lights as he searched for someone else who looked like they could provide a warm bed.

He just had to turn on his charm. Smile, laugh, get hot and bothered easily, and cling to whatever love he could imagine radiating off a person. But not Loukas. The boy was unwell, and Hide was no better.

He found some cheap pills that he hoped were molly mixed with something and was ready to have the best night possible. It was not long before he found what looked like a decent target. At least she looked pretty from the back, anyway.

He sat down beside the girl and gave her a good look. Not his type. Too scrawny and her ass was too flat up close. He preferred them with a lot more meat on their bones, but Hide was done for anything at this point. He just needed to wait for the full effect of the drugs to kick in and it would not matter what the dumb bitch looked like.

He heard the glass clink and teased, "Well, aren't you a cutie? You alone tonight?"

The girl swiftly turned around, and Hide wanted to scrub his mouth out with soap.

"Excuse me?" At that moment, he began to regret every choice had ever made due to what it all led to. His worst nightmare. "Hide?" Carole said with disgust.

"Argh, fuck!" Hide hoped lightning would strike him down and he could rest in peace.

"What are you doing here?" Hide gawked.

Then he noticed the sign.

Ladies' night, ½ off.

Oh.

She squinted at him, noticing what he was looking at before shaking her head. "Figures here was where you ran off to. Makhi told me about it. What are you doing here?"

"None of your business, hag. I'm having the time of my life." Hide's gaze went to the three empty glasses. She could lie as much as she wanted but he

CHAPTER 11

wasn't blind. He had to proceed with this as cautiously as he could. "How did you get here? Or know that I was even there in the first place?"

"I asked Makhi to drive me." She grumbled,"Not a fan of that bike, and the answer to your second question is, he told me where you go after, in his words, getting clingy and upset with everything."

Hide flinched at how Makhi thought about how he reacted. He knew Hide was upset, and probably was well aware he just wanted someone. . . Anyone.

However as usual, like everyone else, Hide was *too much*, so why bother with him?

The sound of glass shattering against the floor interrupted his troubling thoughts.

"Hope you can pay for that."

Hide wanted to tell her to jump off a bridge, he could break and throw whatever glass he wanted. The bartender was focusing on another group breaking something themselves, so he couldn't even receive that familiar negative attention he wanted.

"He must have ignored your breakdown, didn't he?"

Hide was prepared to show her a real breakdown if she was gonna keep talking shit. However his aggression was quelled when he paused to observe the girl carefully.

There were several types of drunks. Sleepy drunks, angry drunks, sad drunks, horny drunks, and the drunks who seemed sober but were clearly not cus they start talking too much.

He vaguely remembered her telling him to breathe when he got like this. Before that bubbling mess of emotion within himself overtook his rational thoughts and words, he, for once, took her advice and calmed down before he did something he'd regret. Thus the beast-kin closed his eyes, took a deep breath, and let it all out of his lungs. Every breath felt like a little bit of anger got chipped away. He was still pissed off, but at least he had a little more control.

Hide, biting down his venom-covered tongue, said, "Okay, fuck this. I don't fucking care about him or any of this crap. Don't you have work tomorrow or something? Rather than shove your nose in my business."

"Hm, I can handle it. I'm not you."

Or was she just an arrogant drunk?

No, screw that. Before this got any worse he was gonna drag her ass out of here.

"No, fuck this. You ain't gonna end up homeless because you want to be stupid. Get your ass up, we're leaving," he said.

Hide snatched her arm, forcing her onto his back. As much as she struggled, Hide knew she could not get away from him.

"I said I'm fine!" she insisted.

"Wow, I believe you fully." Hide rolled his eyes. "I bet you can walk just fine. Maybe even drive us to the boardwalk for one last look at the sea."

"I don't want your hands on me, you know."

"Well, should have thought of that, darling, before distracting me from my night for no reason," Hide sneered as he stomped his way out. He pulled out his phone to call a cab while he ignored the spots that appeared in his vision.

He was doing well.

"My reason was a fluffy man was going to get himself into something he'll cry about later, " Carole said. Hide was fully ready to tear into her for that remark until he was hit with the strong odour of the booze on her breath. He hoped she would not vomit on him again.

"I just wanted to get a dumb girl to fuck and dump. Instead, I got you. Thanks for that," Hide said, noting the taxi stopping close by.

"Creep. Probably high school with how young your partners are getting."

"Shut the hell up."

Hide would normally have said more, but he was aware she was wasted, so there was no point.

As he ran over the cab, he felt something wet slide down his neck. "What the hell are you doing?"

"Just tired. And where are we going?"

Hide let her slur on him. Drool was over his neck as they got into the vehicle.

Figures.

"Somewhere not here," he said.

CHAPTER 11

He pointed to where he wanted the driver to go and he could already tell his hard-earned pocket change had gone to waste.

He just had to lie low for a few days, avoiding that cat until then.

What a pair he and Carole were.

"Okay, so what were you even planning to do in there, other than getting yourself in something you'll beg for help for later," she muttered.

"Oh, you know, having a good time, getting bitches, making them fuck my face as they beg for my fat cock. The usual."

Hide emphasised each word of his potential escapades and included every detail possible. It was all rewarded by the twitch of the woman's lip.

Disgust was what he revelled in, and if he could break through her smug exterior, it was a win.

There was an open silence as the engine of their ride rumbled. Hide groaned and poked his head out the car window, seeing the long line of traffic before them.

He turned to the girl and suspected that she might be sleeping.

Or resting her eyes.

Maybe he could just babble to pass the time.

"You know, I learnt a few things. One of them is funny. Want to hear? No? Then fuck you. Makhi doesn't love me. You knew already? Great, I'm happy to now join your little club of 'no one loves Hide.'" He couldn't help but let out a dry laugh, not caring if she even heard a single word from him. The cab driver probably didn't give a damn. "I told him how I felt, gave him a little smooch and he . . ." Hide stared at the city lights and could not stop the burning in his chest. ". . . didn't like it and never liked it. I kinda knew that, but I just hoped something would be different. He knew I just . . . I just wanted him to touch me. Not even sexually, just anything. I just wanted him to let me know I'm important in his life, and he just ignored it. Cus I'm apparently too damn much for him!"

He glanced over at Carole's frail structure. A weak part of him was desperate for affection, even from her. Maybe when she was awake, he could beg her for it. He did that with Makhi when they were both drunk, and it did not make him feel better. Maybe that would be how he gets her off his back. He could make her know she's wasting her time as his friend and he doesn't care about her. He never wanted to anyway . His time with Makhi when he begged only made that hole even deeper. He just no longer wanted to care about these morons.

Hide remembered Xander telling him that he was just selfish who only cared about people when he got something out of it. As much Hide hated the guy, he already knew that. However, Xander thought it was because he wasn't putting up with his BS so Hide was only his boyfriend for shelter. He was wrong, Hide was his boyfriend because he used to love him. The beast-kin wanted that attention no matter how much of a monster that man was to everyone else. He knew what he was yet for him he would ignore it all.

Hide scratched his cheek as the feeling of several threads growing on it grew more intense. There were eyes on him as the cab came to a stop and he dragged the girl to her apartment. In hindsight, he should not have taken anything, especially from someone he knew was sketchy. Hide was aware he got too touchy when on something.

He would get so desperate, pining after someone who probably did not feel the same, and never had felt the same.

Shit, maybe there was something else in it.

The spots grew in numbers and it almost seemed like it covered the world with glitter. Hide grit his teeth and picked Carole back up on his back.

He had to keep talking to the girl as they came up to her door. He just needed to keep saying things. "So Makhi doesn't like me like that, but you know who does in this fucked up world? Yup, the college guy, and I sucked his dick. He was an asshole during it too, so I was mad as hell. And you know what happened after? It's even more hilarious, a knee slapper if you will."

His chest felt tight.

"He kissed my cute little face. And I decided to of course ghost that creep." He flopped the girl on the apartment couch.

The colours of the room were too bright in his eyes. Everything seemed to bend and wave.

Why him?

"Why does this happen?" he muttered.

CHAPTER 11

Hide could feel the eyes of quite a few too many around them, probably staring at them like they were crazy. He began unconsciously scratching at his skin as the feeling of threads transforming into worms spread all over him as they now crawled over his skin.

The girl's face swirled as she groaned, "Hide, ouch. I can hear. Just slow down for a bit."

Hide's breathing grew shallow. His chest felt like a cage was constricting him.

"Makhi said you were rambling about someone called *boss* when you were with him and panicking and—"

This was not a good time. Why remind him of that name he had tried so hard to forget now?

The man who was obsessed with him as a kid and loved what he was.

He saw his horns and found him so cute.

He was lonely and desperate.

"I . . . I have to go," Hide muttered. He could not breathe.

It was his fault.

It was always his fault.

He could not keep a relationship because of what he was. He wanted to stay with that man in his house. Hide was such a flirt back then, too. That was what may have happened. As *Alex* said, it was in his nature to do so.

"Hide, Hey! Where are you going!"

Hide did not know where he was or what he was doing. The lights were bright and the whirl of the ceiling fan was too loud and his bitten tongue tasted of rusty metals.

Hide then felt his head hit against the door frame of her apartment door and he passed out.

For a long while, he felt at peace, swimming in the infinite darkness.

But life was not so easy, and that tranquillity didn't last for long.

When he opened his eyes saw a pair of purple staring back at him, his back propped up against a pillow, the light from the bulb above burning his retinas.

Carole looked relieved, as if she was glad he had not choked on his tongue in his sleep.

The two stared at each other for who knew how long until he said, "Why do you keep doing this with me?"

Carole shrugged. "I can ask the same. Over and over."

He did not want to think about why he panicked again for no reason. He just focused on the girl in front of him, who held his hand tight. She squeezed at certain intervals, creating a somewhat soothing rhythm.

"You're focusing on me, right?"

"Yeah and your dumb ugly face," he said, as the tightness in his chest lessened.

Hide deep down knew if he finally put his foot down and told her to stop drinking, she may do it. As difficult as it was, he knew she could do it.

Unlike him.

That was the reason he had not told her. The knowledge that someone so similar to him would no longer need him scared him more than anything else.

"You had an anxiety attack."

"Thanks, Captain Obvious. Anything else on the Redundancy News Network?" Hide groaned, laying back on the couch. He glared at nothing, but he hoped it was hurting someone. "When did yours stop, anyway?"

"I don't have them," she said. He noticed she shifted uncomfortably.

He could still see the faint scarring on her body.

He never got why some people wanted kids around but despised them that much. He could never understand it and he hated children. Loukas made him wonder why people could still hold love for people who only hurt them. Wonderful memories or not, the pain outweighed every happy memory he had with his own guardian. He couldn't comprehend holding any type of positive thought about them, like Loukas seemed to do.

He felt nauseous even thinking of it.

Carole sat by his side, Hide saying nothing back and leaning into her proximity. He was grateful to know she would not touch him, and she was probably feeling the same.

"I need a fat girlfriend right now."

He heard the girl snort. "You don't."

CHAPTER 11

"Why not? I'm single, ready to mingle, and on the market 24/7." He gave a humourless laugh. "I hate being alone."

"Hide, you're not as smart as you think." Carole was staring off at something. "You're not alone, anyway."

"Aren't you sentimental?" Hide chuckled.

"Don't push it."

"Fine, whatever, Carly Warly." Hide gave some thought and asked, "What do you think of Loukas, then? He's a loser, but he seems like the last person to be less alone, you know."

He could hear the woman sigh. "I don't know a thing about him other than from you, so take what I say with a grain of salt. Maybe some people are just made to be alone."

"Lame, you read that in a fortune cookie?"

He hated how his friends talked about the man. She was right, but none of his friends knew Loukas like he did.

If Loukas was meant to be alone, then what a miserable existence he had.

"Carly, can I have my phone for a bit? I need to check on something," Hide asked.

Carole seemed a bit tired, and muttered, "I'm not your mother. Just keep it down."

"Fine, it ain't like I'm gonna scream into it. Just get some rest, alright."

"Sure, we'll see about that," she grumbled.

Hide glanced at her, noting how she quickly drifted off. He still found it impressive she was so functional as a drunk with her big stupid concern, but that was not the point.

He looked at his phone, scrolling through the many messages sent between him and Makhi as he remembered his desperation around the guy. No wonder Makhi had enough. Hide was always a wishy-washy asshole, no question about it.

Yet reading these messages and reflecting on the past year had put a thought in his head. He had been nothing but a jackass to someone as sensitive as Loukas, yet that young man would always hold him so highly no matter what he did.

He leaned into the girl's ear hoping she wasn't too deeply asleep and whispered, "Carly?"

Her face scrunched up at his voice and she said, "Hm? What?"

"Can I stay here for a while?"

"Sure. Just don't shout so much."

"Thanks, and don't nag me and we'll be fine."

She passed him a glare, and he grinned at her.

Hide closed his eyes as he thought back to this summer.

What a long season it had been.

CHAPTER 12

Loukas allowed himself to stay within the safe sea of darkness.

He had no desire to escape it, much less able to.

No matter what he tried, he always felt like he was drowning under a thick layer of viscous fluid coating his body in a never-ending vat of oily slime. It filled his mouth with a vile sludge and plugged his ears. He sunk further and further into the void, where he could not scream. All he could do was sink below the surface.

How long had it been since he started falling?

An hour?

A day?

Maybe even a week . . .

But one thing he knew for certain was that he was falling deeper, and he was happy.

Excited, even.

Maybe this was what he truly wanted in the end. All he had to do was fall.

His body slammed hard on the unforgiving ground. In some form of twisted mercy, he did not die. Loukas found himself face down on a gross, grimy mattress as the cold basement bit his fingertips.

He forced his heavy eyelids to lift, allowing peeks of light in. The sudden brightness burned worse than directly staring at the sun. He swiftly shut them again and stayed within the safe confines of darkness.

His head spun and throbbed with pain as if someone had slammed a hammer against his skull, opening it up from the inside. He attempted to open his eyes again and found a haze of red had clouded his vision. Loukas wanted to go home, take a painkiller, and stay in bed for the rest of the day. It would be difficult, with his limbs feeling like lead.

The fog in his vision cleared, revealing the bright and irritating fluorescent bulb above him. It was still agonising but at its usual level of discomfort.

His eyes had always been too sensitive to light.

Loukas winced once he felt the firm foam mattress against his back, then realised just how sticky it was from some sort of fluid.

The tall man, with as much effort as he could, lifted his arm from the ground to search his pockets. As groggy as he was, he did not want to deal with thieves or the possibility of being injured.

Uncle had warned about all the horrors that could happen if he flashed his wealth around. He found his usual itinerary of items: his wallet, his keys, and his phone all in their rightful place.

He sighed with relief, but that left an important question unanswered.

Why was he here?

Why could not he remember anything?

His mind tried to recollect the memories whirring in his mind as the warehouse basement came into sharper focus.

He went to visit Xander, then . . .

Loukas felt his head throb again. He raised a hand to his forehead to feel sticky blood.

Now wide awake, Loukas' mouth was filled with sweet blood. His clothes now clung to his body like damp, over-soaked rags. The odour of blood, piss, and vomit assaulted him.

It all came rushing back.

A week full of blood, the pleasure of it all over his body flooded his mind. The screaming filled his ears, sending nothing but a delirious ache of desire through him.

His gaze was on a body of a rat beast-kin carved up like a pumpkin with insides scooped out in and left on the ground as an unrecognisable slurry.

CHAPTER 12

Loukas tried not to think hard about some of the sticky mess he was feeling in his pants and what he had done.

He knew what happened and he could only feel numb towards it. Not the deranged, feverish thrill or the soul-crushing self loathing.

That emptiness was the worst thing he had felt in a long time.

"You're up already?" Xander chimed, walking into the room and wiping a few scalpels and knives with alcohol.

Loukas noticed under his arm was the camera, full of every activity they had done. According to the man, he made sure neither of their faces would show up on film.

"W-why do you . . . record it?" Loukas asked, not even sure if he wanted to know, but he just needed to know why.

Xander cast him a glance and said, "I make a lot of money from these and for personal use. Trust me, there are many people like you out there."

"I . . . I want to go home now," Loukas said. He hated looking at the body. He heard Xander tut and pat his hair.

"Well, your stay is almost over, but shouldn't you clean up first? You're hungry, right?"

Xander accepted his sickness, even to the point of enjoying watching him. Maybe that was the reason such a person wanted someone like Loukas. What else he had, other than his curse? Nothing else about him mattered to both his family and the society he had tried so hard to be normal around. He was a boring person outside of his illness that has made him an abnormality in need of a cure. However, that affliction was wanted.

He tried not to think about Xander's encouragement during that night. The vague memory of the blond behind him 'helping' him move rhythmically in and out of the bisected torso was one he felt oddly numb about. In fact, Loukas felt detached from it all, like it was just a film he had finished watching. A film with an actor that looked like him because the real Loukas would not have been able to be so bold on camera, especially for the kinds of people Xander sells those movies to.

Now that he thought about it, he had eaten none of their victims. Loukas had only bitten and spat out their parts because deep down, he did not want to reward himself like this.

"Loukas..." The way Xander said his name was so harsh, Loukas did not want to hear him say it again. So, with a weak smile, he nodded.

"I'll try."

Loukas picked up the body, and he salivated at what was before him.

"Can't even help yourself. It's fine, I enjoy watching," Xander encouraged.

Loukas glanced back at his friend and said, "I... We can put him with the rest of the bodies."

Xander's smile faltered at his request. "Well, start digging in the back. You can handle that by yourself, right?'"

Loukas gave him a nod and picked up a shovel. He stared down at his hands during the process and noticed a slight difference in them. His fingernails felt sharper now, like a carnivorous beast-kin's claws than human fingernails.

He would cut those later.

Loukas came back to the room, taking some of the cleaning solution that Xander got in advance. He did ask the demon where he got that and all it got was a smile and a soft chuckle. Xander just said he bought it like everything else and Loukas felt stupid for asking.

He bit his bottom lip in embarrassment as he dampened the rag in the solution and began scrubbing at the bloodstains. He tried to focus on the soft hiss that occurred once the solution made contact with the stain, allowing for the rise of blood bubbles, lifting away the filth. It was better than potentially dealing with the conflicting emotions and thoughts that whirled around in his brain. .

Xander sat by and watched him carefully, curious yet still not so readable.

"You know you would not be so hungry if you ate. Resisting this much is strange when you know what happens when you don't eat," he said.

"I know," Loukas replied.

"Then why? You killed them already and desecrated their bodies afterwards, anyway. Why don't you eat them?"

"I... I just don't know." Loukas' hands shook. He was aware of the hypocrisy of his actions. He could pleasure himself with the bodies, kill them and mutilate them while he orgasmed, but could not bring himself to feed on

CHAPTER 12

them.

Maybe there was this invisible line he saw. A line that once he accepted that part of himself, there was no going back.

To eat was his first type of gratification, one that always linked with the sin of lust. If he willingly ate for the sake of eating he would have taken away his one form of self-punishment. He would lose this agony of hunger, and he did not want that. He needed that pain and shame.

A life without it, especially now when even acting on his urges brought none of that previous guilt and disgust, was terrifying.

Loukas finished cleaning up, and Xander clapped at his accomplishment.

"Well done, Puppy." Xander grabbed Loukas' chin, his hand drifting down his stomach. His finger tugged at the hem of the young man's shirt. "I can give you a reward."

His hand slipped underneath the fabric as Loukas' breath quickened. He wasn't sure what to say to the person now trailing his fingers over his pale scar-ridden flesh. He felt a heat grow within his body as those digits moved upwards pressing against a nipple, the other remained near his groin just above his waistband.

"You're so soft but so rough. Is there something wrong, Puppy?" Xander's voice was jovial, making Loukas second guess his own discomfort.

"St—" Loukas' throat and mouth felt dry as those hands caressed his sensitive skin. He wanted to tell Xander about his mounting unease with his touches, but Loukas didn't want to make his host feel bad. Xander had been nothing but kind to him so far, so he should just be grateful. His temporary anxiety was a minor thing, after all.

"You're such a good boy." The shameful heat immediately pooled to his lower body. His dick throbbed when he heard those wonderful words. "Just a handsome, obedient boy. You cleaned up so well. Probably wanted my full attention with how good of a job you did."

The hesitation that emerged immediately crumbled, and Loukas didn't care that he moaned at the praise. His pants felt too tight and he needed to hear more.

"It's almost pathetic that you want a man to touch you this much." Before

Loukas could comment on what seemed like an insult, that hand travelled and palmed his erection, drawing a whimper out of him.

"This already got hard when no one has even touched it? I was just expressing my admiration for you." He leaned into Loukas' ear and whispered, "Were you going to touch yourself if I hadn't noticed how turned on you got from just my embrace?"

Loukas couldn't respond. As much as he wanted to tell Xander he wasn't going to do any of that, or at least thought he wasn't, none of that mattered with how turned on he was. Loukas' false show of resistance turned to submission, moving his hips against Xander's hand for the friction he desperately needed. Wasn't this what he wanted? A touch from a man so kind. Someone whose full attention was on him, fully understanding what he was and what he liked.

Loukas couldn't hold back his moans at such a service. His tendril emerged from his back, as if to show Xander exactly what he truly desired. They slithered and wrapped themselves over their owner's sensitive body, who had now crumpled to the floor, wanting more.

The demon chuckled at the young man's poor attempts of dealing with his lust. He flicked away one squirming red tendril caressing his neck. Those lips were kept close to Loukas' ear and said, "Say thank you to your daddy for noticing your needs. Was that what you were about to call me?"

What?

"I-I . . . I don't know what you're talking about."

Loukas stared at the demon gritting his teeth, but it was very obvious that despite his mortification and degrading comments, he was only more aroused. The tentacles movement grew more lively.

"Oh, you love to play innocent. You know I prefer Sir or Master, if you're willing. That's why I didn't touch you. I know what you like, and I'm fine with you being so adorably pathetic. Get rid of those things since I prefer to solely care for you right now."

That word came out of the demon's lips again. It made Loukas want to falter in shame and at the same time feverishly grind against something to relieve the now-unbearable throbbing between his legs. With that command,

CHAPTER 12

his assistance retracted back into his body, leaving him with only one who would let him finish.

Xander would not go further than this unless Loukas begged for him as his preferred title. For once, Loukas finally looked the man in the eye. Instead of kindness, care, maybe even the love he craved, Xander looked at him with hunger. Pure lust at a brand new toy he had received. Before the man could say anything, Xander pulled his hand away, much to Loukas' frustration.

The boy let out a whine that the blond ignored. "But I know you prefer the non-living. Let's get you home, okay?"

No, please, let me cum, Sir . . .

That was about to slip from Loukas' mouth before reason took hold and he stopped himself.

Loukas gave a strained smile in response instead. "I . . . okay . . . I would like that. Give me a moment."

He allowed Xander to take his hand. The man's face was gentle as he helped Loukas to his feet."Hmm it's a shame you start school so soon."

"Oh. . ." Loukas had almost forgotten about that. In his time spent with Xander and Hide the return to routine had been the furthest thing from his mind.

Xander chuckled and prodded a finger into his chest. "For a treat, I can drive you back to my place to get you all packed up. Maybe a little cup of tea together for old times sake."

Loukas quietly nodded while he tried to not think too much about what had just happened. That hunger disappeared and was replaced with that familiar gentleness he didn't want to lose. Loukas wanted to push it away as just him being paranoid, but as he sat by the older demon on the way home, the unease never left.

***

"Well that seems to be everything, my lovely Puppy." Xander chuckled at their quick work with his luggage already neatly packed and placed near the elevator door. His clothes were all washed and ironed to a neat, spotless perfection as if he hadn't been doing so many sinful things in them. Loukas sat on one of Xander's expensive leather couches in just his pyjamas as his host insisted that Loukas just relax while he took care of everything else. The hot milky ginger tea warmed Loukas' core.

"Um, thank you Xander."

"You're welcome, Puppy." Xander stirred some sugar into his tea. Before he could say anything else, Xander then said, "I hope you have a good semester. Boys, like you, need all the help they can get for classes."

"Yeah. . ." Loukas knew once he left through that elevator, he would be alone again. Back to how he was at the very beginning of his summer holiday.

"Is something wrong?"

Loukas was a bit caught off guard with Xander's concern, but he couldn't ask for anything better. He wanted to ask him if he could stay here with the demon, but something caught in his throat. Why was he so hesitant about this? He didn't want to be alone but at the same time, that look Xander gave him never left his mind as it made its way through every vessel in his body.

"Puppy. . . you're shaking."

Loukas jolted and saw the blond right by his side, hand on his thigh.

"I. . . C-can I st-stay with you?" Loukas muttered, ignoring how Xander's hand made him feel as it inched up his thigh. He should be happy Xander was so fond of him, what right did he have to be uncomfortable?

There was a deafening silence that followed his request. It made Loukas squirm in his seat worried he may have said something wrong. Finally Xander said, "Live with me? You're so sweet." Loukas gently exhaled and was somewhat calmed that it wasn't a straight rejection. The demon chuckled, "So nervous."

"I . . . s-sorry . . . I just was not sure you would want that and I—"

"No no, I understand. I just wish to know why you're so desperate to live with me?"

"Y-your. . . I—" He didn't want to leave and be alone. Hide ran away and once the summer was over, Loukas would have no one.

"I see, how about a game? If you win, you get to visit me every afternoon for our little *hobby* together." Xander had an arm around Loukas' shoulder.

CHAPTER 12

That wasn't what he wanted, he just wanted to not be alone."If you lose, I prefer you to get out of my sight."

Loukas baulked at what he just heard. His host still had his smile, a gently loving face that betrayed what was just said. Loukas didn't want to only visit for their activities, but to be casted away was much worse.

"You don't want to play with me, Puppy?" His name oozed an irresistible sweetness and Loukas just couldn't refuse.

"Okay, yes, I want to see you again. I don't . . ." Loukas looked towards his feet. "I don't want to be a burden."

"Excellent. Let's start." Xander licked his lips. "Now close your eyes and don't open them until I tell you to and stay very still no matter what."

Obeying, Loukas did as asked. Hide used to play games with him too. When he looked back on those times, it was obvious they were just Hide's ways to get Loukas to open up. Just when it felt like hours, he nearly recoiled when strange hands were all over his body. They roamed over his torso, caressing every inch of skin covered in cloth. Loukas bit his lower lip in an attempt to keep quiet and stifle his internal objections.

"You really are a good boy." Was a soft whisper in his ear and Loukas kept still, even as those hot fingers slipped under his shirt to touch his skin and rough scars. It was exposing to have his scarred body felt up the first time. Now this was the second touch he allowed it to happen and Loukas felt like he was being flayed. That damaged tissue was private, something that should and only would be known and felt by him and him alone. But that boundary was crossed and someone was prodding at it, every touch making his chest tighter and his anxiety escalating to a full alarm. Every instinct wanted to kick Xander away from him, but the fear of losing this game triumphed over that primal desire.

Those digits gradually felt less like human fingers and more akin to spider legs caressing over his body. The insect's bristles scraped against his scarred skin, sending a confusing shudder through his body.

Please stop...

"You know, I've met many men in my time, and you are the most special of them." Xander's voice made him hot and dizzy. The praises given made

Loukas internally beam, yet something about this felt like a sticky slime over his soul. Just as he was able to push away the thoughts of Xander's hand touching him, he gasped at the wet kiss on his neck accompanied by a sharp nip tugging his pale skin.

"You moaned at just that? Must be sensitive there. No wonder you pleasure yourself so often, must have wanted that for a long time" His chuckle was deep, and Loukas still tried to play the game keeping his eyes closed. He was not sure how Xander knew any of that but, did he want this? This touch made him more alert, hot but at the same time nauseous. Maybe he did want this. Loukas knew what was going on but didn't know what to do.

"So, sweet Puppy, will you *perform* on camera for me? I want to see your full face this time. As you enjoy the embrace of a nice older man I found. He looks quite a bit like your uncle, so I know it may help your passions."

Loukas wanted to say no.

"I want to hear you say 'Sir' the whole time. Isn't that what you always wanted, my sweet dog?"

He needed to say no but if he did that, what else was there for him?

". . . okay."

The uncomfortable molestation finally stopped and in the dark, he was given what he craved, a sweet gentle hug.

"Thank you, I'm so proud of my sweet Puppy."

Loukas leaned into the embrace, enjoying the temporary warmth before the depravity he would do to entertain his host one last time. He kept his eyes closed, knowing that if he opened them, Xander would look at him the same way Loukas looked at the men he brutalises.

Entertainment, that was what he was to Xander, but he didn't mind that. Loukas was thankful Xander wanted him around and treasured what he could give. If he was loved for only that reason, then he would be the best one Xander could ever have.

The demon understood his interests, and was someone who could take control. Loukas was his precious Puppy and he was happy to finally be so important to someone.

Loukas threw up that night and scrubbed away at his skin.

CHAPTER 12

***

Thus, the summer came to a close and Loukas signed a new lease, allowing him to come back to his now very familiar off-campus housing. A place where he could be with his plants, thankful well cared for in his absence, and with his new friend in his contacts.

The much older man offered him a trip the following summer across the country, which still surprised Loukas.

He internally debated on whether he would take the offer. As much as the romantic idea of travelling sounded to him, something in his gut still felt sick at the idea of travelling alone with Xander. He was still nauseous thinking about that 'game' they had played. The actual act of desecration of the dead was the least upsetting thing about it.

He pushed those feelings aside and tried to accept the hand that had reached out to him.

Classes would not start for another week, but that was fine. It gave him more time to pull himself together.

Ah, of course.

In the little corner at the back of the closet, he placed the many trinkets he had gathered over the summer. A tuft of black hair, an old chewed up gum, a Q-tip he saw Hide toss on the side walk, and many printed photos of his beloved.

The man stepped back, admiring all he had collected. Every picture, every piece of his loved one was now before him, organised neatly. He could practically smell the cheap perfume Hide probably wore. It was his greatest piece of art, and Loukas could not help but get on his knees at the grand display of his love.

Disgusting, no wonder he wants nothing to do with you.

He was terrible.

***

Loukas sank into the water of his newly installed bathtub, enjoying the hot water against his skin.

He spotted a piece of steel wool.

If he could easily take it and scrub it against his skin to clean himself off, he would have done so without a second thought. The rough cloth was not enough to remove his sin when he was staying with Xander. He wanted to do more horrible things, so might as well add a bit more punishment if he was going to keep doing it.

He was so filthy, after all. He stared down at his healing fingernails that he'd recently bitten. They were angry, blistering red from his recent attempts to rid them into non-existence. Every time they kept growing back into claws, never again resembling human fingernails.

He lay in the tub trying to not think of anything before he was interrupted by an incoming call.

He sighed, glad Xander was calling before he proceeded with his plan.

He picked up the phone and said, "Hello?"

"Loulou, hey are you doing anything right now?"

That voice.

Hide was . . .

"Hide?" Loukas almost jumped straight out of the tub only to hear a chuckle.

"Yeah, it's me. Yeah . . . I just wanted to ask if I could come over."

Loukas' throat was dry.

No.

Tell him no.

You are a killer, murderer, and a degenerate.

And he abandoned you.

"Um . . . I'm not sure now's a good time." Loukas squeezed his pendant.

"I know. Listen, I'm sorry for how I acted, alright? You are just . . . I should know better. I fucked up hard with you."

"No Hide, it's not that." Loukas felt his chest tighten.

Tell him, tell him what a perverted corpse fucker you were this summer. How you put your seed into the neck of a body in front of another man. He would love to hear about how much practice you've been having for his living body.

Tell him how much you need Xander for your urges. And your shrine you made from stealing his things.

Imagine if he was not around.

You feel just so hungry right now.

"Loulou, I don't care. You can pull as much bullshit as you want, but I will bring my ass over to you whether you like it or not, and that's final."

He was so demanding, and Loukas felt his breath catch in his throat.

"I..."

"Bean pole, what time are you comfy?" Hide asked softly. "We need to talk, okay? Both of us need to talk."

Reject.

End it.

The two words rolled over and over in his head until one phrase peeked into his head.

I want him right now. I want him so badly.

"Okay... this afternoon."

Loukas knew he would regret this, but then an idea crossed his mind.

It was a thought that had always been at the back of his mind, but he always suppressed. His desire was now reality, it surfaced in all its glory.

I want to hurt you badly right now, Hide. Maybe I can have you right here for all I want to do with you.

Let me taint every part of you with myself so you can never leave for anyone else. Forever unclean like me.

That was what he desired.

CHAPTER 13

Hide knew he had a mess of a life.

He was aware that he was not as young as he wished, no matter how hard he tried to fake it. As the years wore on, it became more and more obvious that things were not the same.

All his old companions had either outgrown the games they used to play, settled down in some job or stable lifestyle or were like Makhi and pulling away from him. The ones who had stayed all annoyed him, but he did not wish to change.

How could he?

"What was wrong with me?" he muttered to himself as he lay on some motel's bathroom floor. The inside of his mouth tasted of something rancid. His skin was sticky and his teeth ached from possibly grinding them together for too long.

What did he take last night, anyway?

He hoped it was not anything with a hangover that lasted days.

He closed his eyes, waiting for the ache to subside as his thoughts went back to Loukas.

A fear he had was his reason for enjoying his time with Loukas. His motivations for having him around. Loukas was the most naïve man he ever met.

He was young and had an obvious unwavering infatuation; however, that

CHAPTER 13

didn't put him off. Hide liked that. Loukas would look at everything he did with awe, as if Hide was the best person in his world.

That worried him.

Carole may have been an emotional vacuum, but even she knew these types of relationships were landmines and would tell him to back off. There was also one big factor that he could not ignore. Not only did he enjoy the attention, he also savoured Loukas' darker traits.

Loukas was a monster.

A murderer and a sick man who could fuck Hide senseless if he were to be helpless underneath him. If Carole knew, she would have swiftly put her foot down and stopped whatever he was doing.

He had lied to Makhi and Carole about where he was going. Hide knew both cared for him in their own way, and did not wish him to come to any harm. Still, he did not want to stay away from Loukas.

Why couldn't he just dislike the boy and get it over with?

It should have been easy to despise that crybaby, psychotic bitch of a man, but Hide could not bring himself to do so. Instead, he pitied him.

Loukas trusted him and saw him as his one and only friend. Someone he placed his faith in and wanted to be around. It was something Hide did not understand at all. In Loukas' eye, he was the one piece of treasure to track down and keep. If Hide told the boy to jump, Loukas would ask how high.

Not one person in Hide's life was like that to him.

It was a sense of power he never had, and Hide could not help but enjoy every second of it. Loukas' monstrous habits were arousing whilst terrifying.

He could kill the goat beast-kin so easily, yet he always held himself back.

Hide wanted that devotion and to have someone that would hurt him and be his everything. If that was a selfish ship to ride, he would be captain of that vessel.

Hide tried to laugh at such a stupid thought but winced at the awful headache gripping his head. Reminding him what he just spent the night doing.

At least that bitch paid. He certainly was skilled at attracting the stupid and gullible.

Hide felt sick as the ache had only grown worse the more he sobered up. Maybe that boy being damn uptight about drugs had a point.

Loukas . . .

That naive, disturbed boy.

Hide should be better, but he could not bring himself to do that. He squinted at the time on his phone and groaned when he saw he had one more hour until he should be at Loukas' place.

Maybe he would lose track of time again and miss it, leaving the young man to wait for a person who would never arrive. At least then he would once again show Loukas what kind man he was worshipping.

A selfish one.

* * *

Hide stood at the front of Loukas' home. The boy's plants displayed their full beauty, dotting the tiny garden with drops of colour amongst the greenery. Hide raised his brow, sceptical of the decor. He decided it would not hurt to observe them some more. He was already late, so a few more minutes wouldn't hurt, anyway.

A rose caught his attention as it still glistened with clear dew. Hide reached out, not paying much attention, and recoiled from the sharp pain of the stem's prick. The goat opened his palm to see the swelling pinpoints in its creases, evidence marking him for his rough attempt to grab. He wondered what would happen if he squeezed the stem even harder. A seemingly innocent looking flower that could make him bleed. Bleed petals of red like the colour of the boy's eyes.

He had always suspected Loukas may have felt more for him ever since they sat together on the rooftop. Hide, however, could not let himself feel the same. Why would he ruin Loukas like that, anyway? The damn kid had a simple first gay crush and should get over it with time. Nothing more to it than that. Yet, here Hide was, doing what he knew would just encourage his bleeding heart.

Hide reached out again, successfully picking the flower without getting

CHAPTER 13

hurt. He twirled the plucked, pretty rose in his hand before he forced his signature smile. A mask that had helped him face the most awful people and disgusting people.

He banged on the door and shouted, "Knock, knock. Guess who?"

Hide scuffed the tip of his light-up sneaker against the steps. They had run out of battery a long time ago, leaving the soles at a consistently dull blue colour. As he waited, he looked at the rose again. He held the stem in such a way it did not prick him no matter how carelessly he waved it. If he wanted to bleed, he could do so of his own accord.

Observing the lovely pink petals, he noted how well cared for these flowers were. Hide was used to plants dying on him, but Loukas could make them thrive and bloom into what was admittedly a beautiful plant.

Maybe Hide was finally understanding the man's enjoyment of these glorified weeds.

His ears twitched at the sound of someone rushing, possibly knocking something over in their haste. It was a few minutes before the doorknob clicked.

Hide's memory went back to the scent of blood and meat that had overpowered him. An odour so strong, anyone else would have thrown up within seconds.

Would he smell that again?

What came to him instead was the scent of lavender floor cleaner mixed with a minor hint of a citrus fragrance.

A nervous, tall boy with red ruby eyes greeted him at the door. Who he had seen covered in the blood of another previously living being. He was also someone who got teary-eyed and begged for release in Hide's mouth. So desperate Loukas was for touch, like the good, well-behaved lad he wanted to be.

Loukas was panting with obvious exhaustion, complete with sweat over his forehead.

Hide noted the boy might not have cut his hair at all these past few months. It had now grown past his ears. The palm tree probably had not been to the barber in a while. Not that Hide minded the look.

Loukas wore a simple long sleeve white T-shirt, grey sweatpants, and plain white socks. Around his neck was the necklace that Hide had never seen him without.

Hide realised this was the first time he had seen the man dressed so casually before. His limbs were long and lean, wrists poking out the sleeves, revealing a few faded scars.

Hide hoped there weren't any new ones hidden underneath his concealing layer of cloth.

"Um . . . I . . . um, sorry, I didn't mean to hold you up. Um, I will put something on, nicer clothes," the sharp-tooth man said once his gaze met Hide.

Hide gave him a shrug and leaned in his doorway.

"Nah, and quit the fucking apologies already," he said. "I get to see that body of yours with less clothing. So a win on my end."

The shy boy predictably blushed as Hide nudged his way past him to enter his home.

It was not like he was lying about that.

Loukas was an attractive man, all things considered. Too much on the lanky side for Hide's tastes, but the boy made up for it with his outright frightening strength.

The goat beast-kin's eyes automatically began glancing around the room in search of any sign of something dead.

"N-no, wait. Sorry, but no shoes. Um, put them near the doorway."

Loukas pointed to a little corner near the door, where three sets of shoes lay neatly in a row.

"Fine, whatever." Hide peeled off his sneakers, socks, and too-warm hoodie, leaving him in his under-shirt and shorts. He turned to the man again to see he was fidgeting with his fingers and kept his eyes on the ground.

"Hey, it's alright to look. Not like I'm nude."

That statement seemed to tear Loukas out of his thoughts. He stammered, "Oh, I was making us something to eat and—alright? You must be hungry."

Hide was about to refuse the offer. He was not here for this kind of thing. He just wanted to put an end to this type of strange relationship they had.

CHAPTER 13

For both their sakes.

That was until he heard his stomach growl and he remembered he had not eaten a proper meal since yesterday.

Hide shrugged. "Fine, I'd like a little snack, anyway. We'll talk after it cuz I'm hungry. And a hungry mouth is an angry mouth."

"Thank you." Loukas beamed with joy and went towards the kitchen.

At least it made Loukas happy.

Hide, now alone in Loukas' living home, glanced around at the potted plants and indoor seedlings dressing the room in green. He noticed that the lights, from a glance, were most likely LED lights rather than the usual light bulbs. Combined with the hoarding of weeds, Hide concluded that Loukas was the tree-hugging male equivalent of a crazy cat lady. But cuter, and as far as he knew, crazy cat ladies didn't have a body count.

"Why do you have so many plants?" Hide, a man of tactfulness, shouted across the room.

"Huh? Oh, I just had a large garden back home, and I liked them a lot . . . They make the room feel less empty, you know?" Loukas said from the kitchen.

"Plants are like your children, then?"

"What? N-no! Never. I would treat my children nicer."

Didn't he treat these weeds nicely already? Hide could not imagine spending over ten dollars on a potted fern.

The boy needed to give himself more credit.

Hide gazed at Loukas' little movie collection and saw the world's mushiest and cheesiest box sets. All with very average girls, like 5s out of 10, falling into the arms of men who may have been a 7, occasionally a 7.5 in terms of fuckability.

Somewhat expected for a repressed, sappy gay guy, but could he at least have better taste?

Not that Hide cared for films or books, but at least he enjoyed a good horror compared to this trashy shit.

He should not dig so much. He needed to end it all now and not make it difficult.

He needed to tell Loukas that this crush was going to hurt them both, that he didn't feel the same.

He should not feel the same.

Lie or not, he had to say that.

He browsed through Loukas' collection to pass the time, finding no "How to Kill People" or "Rosemary's Baby" type media. Only more bland romances of mediocre flour people. In the back of the cabinet was a box set that looked fairly new. It was the only one with two guys on the cover.

The "Burning Heat: Limited Edition" box set. Was this what people liked nowadays? Probably sappy nonsense, so Hide wasn't bothering with it.

"It's ready!" Loukas said from across the room. Hide put the box back in its place and pulled himself off the floor.

"I'm coming, I'm coming, sheesh."

Grilled cheese sandwiches cut into cute little triangular shapes were on the kitchen table.

"Sorry, I can't eat that," Hide said as soon as his eyes landed on it.

"Oh, s-sorry. It's plant-based—Field Roast, so it's not really cheese," Loukas said, rubbing the back of his neck.

"I'm not five, you know," Hide retorted with a raised brow. He took a chair and picked up the sandwich cautiously.

"S-sorry."

"Tsk, what did I say about apologies?"

"Not to? Oh yeah, y-your drink."

"Apple juice with ice. Nothing fancy." Hide sniffed the food and once he assumed it was safe enough, took one bite.

Hm.

Fairly creamy, buttery, and pretty good. Hide was usually not a fan of substitute stuff, but Loukas seemed to know how to make these things well.

It was delicious, savoury, and hit all the right notes for a sandwich. Before he knew it, Hide devoured the slices as Loukas came back with his drink, which he grabbed and chugged down to wash down the meal.

The tart flavour of fruit filled his mouth, complementing the toasted meal filling his stomach. When Hide looked up, he noticed Loukas had been

CHAPTER 13

smiling the whole time as he ate. He wished Loukas would keep that smile more often.

"You like it?" Loukas asked.

"It was okay," Hide said. "What about you? You're eating?"

Loukas fidgeted with his hands. "I don't want to eat food most of the time. So it's fine."

Now that Hide thought about it, he noticed the man had repeatedly refused to eat in his presence. Hide would have thought it was to do with his not being a human being. However, now he wondered if it was something beyond that.

"Why? Can't eat human or—" Hide cut himself off, realising how tactless his question was.

He noticed the younger man still flinched at the statement and said, "I can . . . I just forgot. I don't need it."

Those scars around his wrists had always worried Hide. Loukas could be starving himself on purpose, too. Hide was not sure about the extent of it, but Loukas not being physically human should not be an excuse for him to treat himself this poorly.

Loukas needed help.

Hide grit his teeth. He should not want to be this close and concerned, yet he was.

He continued, "Dude, no need to worry around me. I mean, we jerked off on call together and you came in my mouth in a restaurant bathroom, so it's not like I'm a judging man."

Loukas turned from worried to embarrassed and flustered in an instant.

"I-I . . . You . . . you're not upset?"

"It's fine!" Hide rolled his eyes. "If it weirded me out, I would have ended that call. I wouldn't have sucked you off or been here if I disliked you that much. "

"I-I never thought about that." Loukas let out a dry chuckle. "It . . . it's all my first time. I've never had a man touch me like you had."

Hide shifted in his seat and wondered if what he was doing was right. There was something sweet about the boy.

The part telling him to end it grew weaker.

"I'm surprised. Babe, you're sexy as fuck, so I'm wondering why only now you have popped your cherry."

"Stop it!" Loukas buried his face in his hands and Hide could not help but laugh.

Almost made him forget how screwed up everything was.

Now to the point.

It was his last chance.

"Loulou, you got the whole world open to you. So I'm wondering what you want with me."

Loukas lowered his gaze. "Hide . . . I don't know."

"Loulou, don't pull that crap on me. That's my thing. You should have a reason."

"You don't know a thing about me."

Hide flinched at the sight of Loukas digging his nails into the table, scraping away the supposedly sturdy wood. That was a contrast to how unsettlingly cold he became, yet Hide had to continue. "Well, fuck me, you don't either. But your edgy bullshit ain't gonna stop me from prodding now." He finally asked, "What would you have done to me that night? When I was on the ground losing blood and you were on top of me."

Loukas stiffened. Although Hide was hesitant, he scooted closer. "Hey, might as well get this over with since I'll be staying with you for a bit. I ain't leaving so early."

"Hide . . . you really don't know how horrible that question is. Even now," the man muttered.

"Even now? What are you talking about?"

"Hide . . . you smelt nice."

It could have been just him, but Hide saw how red the man's eyes were.

How long had he not eaten?

Loukas' hand was on his thigh. His breath was hot. "I learnt a lot about what I want this summer. If you were on the ground right now with an open stomach . . . I would shove my penis in there and fill it up with everything I ever wanted to give you. Make you sticky with my admiration for you. If you

CHAPTER 13

were still alive despite all I've done, it would only excite me. I would then heat up one of the knives on the gas stove and shove it up your ass and make love to you with that. Mutilate your pure body as it roasts and rips you apart from the inside.

"I would make sure it lasts as long as possible to allow you to scream in ways no one else has ever made you scream. Only I would be blessed to hear such a beautiful sound, and I would make sure no one else would take that from me. I want to worship you at the end of it all so I would eat your flesh until there's nothing left, not even bone."

Hide opened his mouth, unsure what to even say to this admission. Where did this come from? It was not a flighty request nor a fantasy that Loukas wasn't serious in doing. Loukas wanted to do all those terrible things to his body out of love. The man's obsession was always strong, but there were no longer any placid attempts at euphemisms. What he just heard was an admittance of desire, empty of any gentleness. The man wanted him dead because he loved him.

Hide knew he had been at least disgusted by that, fearful of who he was sharing the room with. A tinge of fear ran down his spine, there was a bite of excitement, anticipation even, on what Loukas would do.

Hide needed to think fast.

"Loulou . . . did something happen to you these past few days?" he asked cautiously.

"A lot . . . so much and you . . . Hide, you make it so hard."

Another line of thought entered Hide's mind.

"Do you want to bite me?" Hide may have been losing his mind, but he might as well lose it his way. "Do you want to show me what you learned?"

He truly loved to play with fire.

Loukas went from his half-lidded eyes of longing to fully alert.

"W-what!" he shouted, a rare thing from the man.

"I said what I said. If you want to taste me, I might as well let you if it calms you down," Hide said.

"I-I . . . oh Hide, you don't get it."

Hide rolled his eyes. The boy could not be serious. He hoped Loukas did not notice his attempt to stop his own hands from shaking.

"I don't get it? Loulou, you're starving yourself."

Hide could not help but allow his eyes to drift towards Loukas' mouth and admire how sharp his teeth were. The boy's fingernails strangely looked more like claws.

How would they feel buried in my skin?

Painful, scary, hot . . .

The red-eyed man licked his lips. His tongue seemed even longer. He could not hide his yearning. Loukas shook his head and said, "H-hide . . . do . . . do you know what you smell like to me every time you're near?"

Loukas picked himself up from his seat and grabbed the goat man by the front of his vest.

"Hey! What the hell are you—"

"Hide, your smell is too much. Some days. Every day as I watch you go home."

Hide, paralysed with fear, could only watch the other man pick him up from his seat with ease. His limbs refused to move and his mouth felt dry. If he was shaking, Loukas didn't notice or care. Before he could think of anything else, he felt the taller man's face in his long curly hair and his hot breath near his neck. The tips of his teeth grazed his flesh, teasing it with their points.

Loukas' tongue, now long and slimy, caressed his cheek. The wet muscle moved to just underneath his eyelid. Hide tried to squirm, but Loukas held him tight as he proceeded to lap at Hide's eye jelly, making the goat squeal at the harsh burning of salvia and roughness against his cornea.

Hide tried to shove Loukas off, but the man was stronger and his grip grew even firmer to taste the now-stinging orb. He heard the man let out a shudder in his ear as his grasp tightened and sharpened claws dug into his shoulders. Loukas burrowed his nose into his hair to sniff him.

Hide managed to shove him away, and he dropped to the tiled kitchen floor.

He scrambled to his feet and glared at Loukas, who gave a dry, humourless laugh. "Th-that's why I don't want to do that. Not with you. I would . . . kill you if I did any of it."

CHAPTER 13

It was like the night he learnt Loukas was a monster, in that his instincts were screaming for him to run away. Every cell in his body knew that this person was something dangerous and could prevent him from potentially seeing another day in this life. Now this predator was giving him another chance to escape, this time unharmed in an act of mercy and instead of doing so, Hide stood frozen as conflicting emotions bombarded him.

Why did Loukas give him, of all people, this kind of mercy? He wanted to do all that horrible shit to him, yet he wasn't doing it. Why tell him all that crap anyway? As much as it terrified Hide, Loukas' admission made his heart race with excitement. He was actually hoping Loukas would lose control at that moment and do as he had said. However, that was not the case, and a confusing frustration was what Hide was left with.

Why this? Why doesn't he just get it over with already?

Among the dozens of answers that flew through his mind, one made its home. Do *I look so weak to him? Maybe Loukas sees me as just weak prey that he just can't bear to hurt.* Hide's fear then transformed into a spiteful rage.

If Loukas thought that shit scared him, he had another thing coming.

Did Loukas pity him?

Did he think that he was just some helpless bitch?

Who the hell did Loukas think he was?

Deep down, Hide knew he was on thin ice. He was in the home of a man who warned him of what he would do the longer they stayed together.

He could run and dodge everything and everyone until he escaped. That was the plan, but another idea drifted into his mind. He was gonna give that boy a feast and show him what kind of delicious devil he was dealing with. Hide had to make his choice.

Hide took a dinner knife off the table and, before Loukas could do anything, sliced the palm of his hand as deep as he safely could. His actions were rewarded by the thick flowing of blood that ran all the way to the tips of his fingers.

"H-Hide, what are you—"

Loukas raised his panicked voice again, something Hide still found unusual to hear from his mouth. And he still yearned to hear more of it.

Loukas cared.

In his fucked up way, he cared.

The sting led to a timely shudder down the goat man's spine. It was not enough to send him over in a dizzying embrace of elation, but enough for a spark to light up within himself.

Loukas stared in horror as Hide sat on the kitchen table with his fingers outstretched.

Hide grinned and crossed his legs, licking his lips. He commanded, "On your knees, baby boy. Don't you want to clean me up, Loulou? You're so hungry, aren't you?"

Loukas' red eyes dilated at the sight of his blood. Hide kept his smug smile. He positioned himself on the table to create a safe distance in case of a quick escape, but that did little to dampen Hide's excitement.

Loukas obeyed without question and was on his knees. In no time, his lips were so close to Hide's fingertips. Hide could feel his hot breath on his open cuts. Loukas' maw opened much wider than any human mouth should, revealing a plentiful cavern of teeth. So many sharp bits of enamel pointing in every direction.

Hide almost jerked his hand back in fear of the mouth snapping down on his digits. He also found himself mesmerised. A hole so slimy, red, wet, and hot.

A tongue lolled out of that cave like a fat, crimson worm. Thick, translucent mucus coated its muscular appearance, similar to the tentacles that sprouted from Loukas' back.

The thing curled around Hide's fingers and kissed his wounds. It swirled around them and grabbed them all with a sharp tug.

Hide sighed at the feeling of the tongue now digging into his open palm. In sheer audacity or suicidal bravery, the goat moved his hand back and forth through that hot, wet muscle.

"Don't be afraid to swallow every drop," Hide said as he dove his blood-covered fingers further inside Loukas' mouth. "And don't bite. It's sensitive," Hide breathed out.

Hide felt the teeth lightly graze his skin as he entered Loukas' hungry jaws.

CHAPTER 13

Two powerful sets of claws held down Hide's thighs as the monster suckled and lapped at his blood. Hide wanted to retreat, but the expression on Loukas' face seemed to be one of drunken worship rather than malice. As if one touch from him would cause the boy to cum on the spot.

Hide licked his dry lips and purred, "Good boy. See? I knew you could do it. You're so sweet and kind to me."

He moved a free hand through Loukas' hair, scratching at the base of his scalp.

The boy moaned and suckled more, going further down Hide's fingers at his encouragement.

Poor thing has such awful gag reflexes, Hide thought as the corners of Loukas' eyes were already watering.

His hold on Hide's thighs strengthened, his claws drawing small wells of blood. The excitement of whether the boy would snap at a better source made Hide rub his thighs together to quell his worsening erection. It was certainly better than his hands, and Loukas had such poor control, he could decide at any moment to tear into a more fulfilling meal.

Hide should not be getting hard at this prospect, but he could not help it any more. It made him horny to hell and back. His cock was already half-mast in his shorts with Loukas sucking him off and the worship of the boy's heavenly tongue.

If he was a worse man, he would drop his pants to give Loukas something more meaty to suck and chew on.

The risk of getting neutered was never more tempting than now.

And Loukas would do it, no questions asked. The young man would blow him without a word, drunk on his blood and desires.

Hide's tail wagged faster when Loukas' sharp fangs began cutting into his fingers, biting harder for more red nectar that his cut palm wasn't giving. He did not care, more blood for Loukas and more of this pleasure to relish.

Soon, Hide could not take it any more. Hide reached into his shorts to stroke his cock in front of the man.

He saw Loukas' eyes widen in his adorable surprise, just the way he liked them. Hide said, "Just a little more. Get a good long look, baby. Keep watching.

I know you like what you see."

Hide no longer wanted to tease himself and just furiously got himself off. His hips bucked into one hand as Loukas kept sucking the other. Loukas clamped down, and Hide moaned at the tantalising pain. The thought of the boy finally ripping his fingers off was not enough for what he truly wanted.

Finally, Loukas pulled away with a gasp; saliva connected his lips to Hide's fingers. Those red eyes were now focused on something else. Where his sharp claws cut into his thigh were nice, long streaks of blood.

He might regret this, but Hide could not resist feeding the boy any longer. He peeled his pants all the way down. "Come on now, don't you want the main course?"

Loukas' clutch loosened as he lowered his face to Hide's thighs, just an inch away from his erected cock. His sweat-dampened orange hair lay flat on his face, concealing his eyes as he panted like a dog. His tongue then dragged across the incisions, digging into a few to widen them and enjoy more from his meal. He drank from his, now even worse, wounds like it was an oasis in a desert.

"Yes that's it, baby, keep going." Hide encouraged the man to lick higher by dipping his fingers into the blood and creating a trail for the man's hunger to follow, until he was inches away from Hide's groin. He might regret this, but Hide had never had been harder than he was at that moment. So his trail traversed his dick, making a spiral going from his balls to the very tip. With his gashed palm, he stroked his cock, slathering it in more blood while watching the boy lick up the aftermath.

"Loulou, I know you're hungry." Hide could have blown his load from watching his eager baby eat. Thankfully, his patience was rewarded when Loukas obediently listened and that long tongue started to worship his cock. Wrapping itself like a vine around his shaft, it wiggled around his balls to suckle every last drop. Hide couldn't hold back his whimpering as he possessed the boy by the back of his head to keep him licking.

"Fuck. Good boy, that's it. Very nice, boy. Perfect, sweet boy." Hide decided to take advantage of that kink of his as the licking grew more vigorous and Loukas' sharp teeth were so close. Hide felt the knife-like points less than an

CHAPTER 13

inch away from his chubby, throbbing dick. He could hear Loukas' breath grow more rapid and Hide remembered what Loukas did when he got this excited.

Loukas liked to bite when he got very horny. If he bit now, those teeth would tear Hide's cock off with ease. Loukas would rip it off as the goat came one last time, thrown into the highest peak of pain. Hide wouldn't mind losing his cock like that. He barely used it except to get himself off.

Hide's increasingly feverish thoughts were cut off when he felt pinpricks on the head of his cock, and that was what finally brought him over the edge. He came on the spot, not caring to give a warning to the young man who immediately pulled away, gagging. Hide's musky seed splattered over Loukas' face and dribbled down his chin.

Hide stared at his work, lifting his fingers to eye level then towards his now-mutilated thighs. A million cuts littered his index and middle fingers. Some were thin and lightly bleeding. Others were open, gaping, gushing wounds of bright red that made the cut on his palm look like a paper cut. Maybe the boy let go just to stop himself from amputating it. His thighs were even worse off with a thick coating of blood covering both of them, every cut open to feed Loukas' insatiable hunger.

Hide placed his bare foot on Loukas' thigh, rubbing it and said, "Was that so bad?"

The man did not look him in the eye as he muttered something under his breath and wiped Hide's cum from his face. Loukas began licking it, cleaning every milky, sticky strand he had gathered, sometimes sucking on his fingers as if it was the most delicious meal he had had in a long time.

Hide's eyes lowered to the lump in Loukas' pants. A mischievous idea arose, and he drifted his foot further up the man's thigh.

"What was that? Did you say something?"

"I . . ." Loukas was brought out of his trance, back to squirm in his seat. "J-just your foot is . . . close."

"See, was that so hard? Just a nice angle to watch you clean up my jizz," Hide teased, wasting no time. He placed a hoofed foot on the lump, forcing a gasp.

"And why do you care that it's so close?" Hide asked, pressing his hoof against it. "It's just my foot."

"H-Hide. It's . . . touching."

Taking advantage of the thin fabric, Hide began to slowly rub the fabric in a circular motion.

Poor boy was waiting for it since he was already moving against it, enjoying the friction.

"Baby, I just thought you've been a good boy and good boys like you need a nice reward."

Hide pressed his foot with more pressure, forcing a sharp yelp from the man.

He was absolutely writhing underneath the foot until Hide stopped his rubbing and kept his foot pressed against the clothed cock..

Loukas, blushing and panting, whined, "W-wait, you stopped?"

"I never said I would continue to rub my foot on you like that. You can pleasure yourself on your own, right?" Hide could not help but enjoy how crushed the man looked at what he said.

"That's . . . cruel," Loukas whimpered.

Still, Loukas was moving underneath him. His breathy noises were occasionally cut off by soft moans as he ground against the beast-kin's foot.

"Good boy, I never thought you would enjoy feet that much," Hide laughed.

Deciding to be a little nice, he placed both feet, encircling the lump, allowing enough room for exactly what the poor boy wanted.

"Nice and fuckable like your nice mouth," Hide said.

Loukas groaned as he moved his hips into the shallow foot hole, thrusting as if it was Hide himself. The young man's movement grew more erratic with each passing second.

The boy looked so needy, rubbing himself into the only thing he was allowed to be in. Hide could not help but enjoy the noises his baby made.

"See, you're doing so well. You're such a smart boy, you know what to do."

It seemed the boy was at his limit already. "Pl-please let me c-cum. Pl-please."

"You can, baby. You just have to work for it a little harder. Let it all out. Do

CHAPTER 13

it for me."

Hide, however, was not a monster and moved his feet in time with the boy until his humping lost rhythm. Loukas finally jolted and arched his hips into his hooves. Hide let his mischievous streak take over and stomped his foot as firmly as he could onto the clothed cock. The shriek was so sweet, though it didn't stop him from coming underneath Hide's crushing foot. Loukas went limp on the kitchen floor, shivering as his soft breaths escaped those peach lips.

Hide felt gradually dampening fabric beneath his toes and took his foot off Loukas' crotch.

He kept his hands to himself and asked, "Feel better? Since I kinda know you're still new to this. You alright?"

The man came back to his senses. His face of animalistic lust shifted gradually to one of flushed embarrassment and exhaustion.

"I guess," he stammered, covering his face.

The guy was still easily embarrassed. Not wanting Loukas to sink back into whatever shame pit his cult taught him, Hide got off the table and gave him a pat on the head and caressed his back.

"You did well, though. I enjoyed helping you get off. So I think you did a good job," Hide said as he noticed Loukas seemed to lean into the touch for more.

"I . . . Thank you . . ." Loukas fidgeted where he sat. Hide hoped gratitude replaced whatever shame he had, at least until he changed out of his now-soaked underwear.

Cute.

Hide shook off that thought and noted Loukas' now-familiar timid demeanour had returned. That was a good thing, right?

He could not leave him like this alone.

The goat felt safe enough to turn his back and wince at the sting from his thighs. He grit his teeth and limped to the sink to wash his bleeding hand under the warm water. He took a damp towel to wash his other wounds, biting his lower lip to hold back the pain. It was no different from when he patched himself up before, the only difference was both he and the perpetrator wanted it.

"Th-the plaster is under the sink," Loukas said, pointing to the white cabinet.

"Thanks," Hide replied, not looking at the man, nor did he comment when Loukas left the room to most likely to change or, at worst, overthink what happened.

Hide pulled out the first aid box and let out a sigh, allowing the warm water and stinging soap to wash over his wounds. He got neatly bandaged up as the thought of what they did flowed through his mind.

Was he even helping Loukas?

Could he consider any of this help?

Loukas was a sick man. There was no arguing about that. Sick and disturbed were the two best words to describe him.

Hide wondered what he could do about it, what he could even say to make it better when it never was better.

He had avoided Loukas for weeks and despite that, the boy's eyes never wavered in their fondness.

If Hide told him to jump, he would ask how high.

If Hide told him to bite, he would ask how hard.

That was the man Loukas was and Hide did not hate it.

He stared at his bandages and wondered what lies he could tell to explain it away. His friends would see this as another poor relationship choice.

Yet, he could not bring himself to cut it off.

Loukas loved him.

Loukas shuffled back into the kitchen in a new pair of pants, making every attempt possible to avoid eye contact.

"Enough with the long face," Hide said, hands on hips.

He had to get the guy out of his head for once. "Let's watch one of your dumb movies, alright?"

Loukas' eyes seemed to light up.

"So you're up for it?" Hide asked.

"Y-yeah, I . . . wouldn't mind."

Hide smirked. "Good, I'll get the popcorn."

There might be ramifications for what he had done, the damage of his hand

CHAPTER 13

one of the mildest.

Hide swallowed his guilt at that thought and set the microwave to two minutes.

For once, he was fine with taking the consequence of his actions.

CHAPTER 14

Loukas could not believe what he had allowed himself to do.

He could have rejected that tantalising sweet red honey flowing from Hide's fingertips. He could have done anything else, but he didn't. Instead, he licked and suckled it.

He drank until Hide brought him to the heights of divinity, unlike anything he had ever felt before. Each time with Hide seemed better than the last, and Loukas only wanted more out of him.

However, he did not kill the little goat, no matter how much he bled in his mouth.

Loukas felt no desire to pounce on his prey's small, helplessly carnal body and take what he wanted. Stripping off his skin and gnawing on his limbs. Instead, he sat obediently and drank from his cup of sanguine fluid.

What Loukas could not control was his darker enjoyment.

His body had burned with desire. His hand wanted to move on its own to chase that feeling. But he did not have to resort to that. Hide was so kind in allowing him his painful reward in the end for being so dutiful to him.

He did not deserve that kindness or his comfort afterwards.

The most baffling thing of all was instead of shaming him, leaving him, or calling him disgusting, perverted, or pathetic, Hide stayed and checked to see if he was okay.

Hide wanted to stay and spend time with him for reasons he could not

CHAPTER 14

comprehend. The goat was in his house and was going to watch a movie with him as if nothing had happened.

Maybe nothing happened and Loukas just had an elaborate, erotic daydream. It would make more sense compared to Hide staying with him.

Maybe it could have been even better than that.

This entire summer with Xander could have been in his head, and Loukas would wake up at his desk with the worst headache he ever had.

One thing certain was the blood forever on his lips and tongue, like the sweetest of fruit, ripened to perfection. And the laundry he had to do afterwards.

"Don't think too much about it," Hide assured as he poured the popped kernels into a big bowl.

Loukas wanted to follow that advice but in their brief window of intimacy, that cheap-perfumed man made him nearly lose his mind.

He was so close to throwing Hide off the counter and slamming him onto the ground. His hair would be messy under him, his vest and shorts dishevelled, and those grey eyes full of fear and unstifled longing.

Loukas would bite the rest of his fingers and claim Hide's mouth with his own.

Loukas knew the depravities he enjoyed, and nothing was stopping him from doing any of them but himself. Xander showed him that.

Deep down, he was a selfish creature.

Hide had so many lovely holes for him to use.

It would be so easy.

Hide knew that now but instead of running away, knowing very well he was not safe, he was in Loukas' kitchen making popcorn.

Hide probably thought his feeding would be a one-time thing. That Loukas would not do it again, that he could fix him and Loukas be a normal person with enough attention.

He was so wrong if he thought that.

"Hey, Loulou, what about . . ."

Loukas was once again brought out of his thoughts by the same man. Hide was on his couch, legs swinging over the edge as he waved a Blu-ray disk in the air, holding a big bowl of popcorn in his lap.

"Wh-what?" Loukas said as he tried to straighten himself on the other end of the leather couch. He must have been staring off into space.

This was all so fake.

Hide rolled his eyes and said, "Movie, now. I saw you got some books of this crap." He lifted a box set displaying the colourful artwork. "I ain't reading any of that, so might as well watch the cartoon version."

Loukas rubbed his eyes as he finally recognised what kind of movie Hide had just lifted.

"N-no, not that one!" the taller man said, trying to snatch it away.

"Why? Is it something an innocent boy like you doesn't want me to see?" Hide's tail wagged with excitement. "Is it a film that would make you hard?"

What would turn off Hide from watching this?

"I-it's um . . . very sweet and sappy, extremely so, and-and my sweetest one."

"Ew," the goat man groaned, dropping it to the ground, much to Loukas' relief.

He had to learn to hide these things.

Why could they not always be like this?

Loukas imagined they would have been a normal couple under different circumstances. A normal loving couple, who laughed and watched movies with one another. Frequently joked and teased each other when the mood struck.

In a better world, Hide would not have his hand slashed and wrapped in bandages.

Maybe next time . . .

Why was he thinking about this?

It was not like Hide would come back again for another visit, anyway.

"What about the best film that came out this year?" Loukas chimed.

"Is it romance?" Hide scrunched up his face in disgust.

Ouch.

"Yes . . ."

"Ew."

CHAPTER 14

Hide sank into his seat as if Loukas had suggested they were going to do a full room cleaning.

"But I can pick one that's good. I'm sure you'll love it," Loukas tried to assure.

Hide side-eyed him and looked even more unenthused and said, "Doubt it."

"Please Hide, I can pick a sci-fi one after."

Hide groaned and peered at the ceiling as if contemplating something.

"You are so lucky you're cute as shit," Hide muttered.

"C-cute?" Loukas said, taken aback.

"Fine, we'll watch your PG porn together."

"No! It's not. It's clean and has a very cute couple."

"You're supposed to make me want to watch, not make me hope I get literally bored to death," Hide said, poking him in the chest.

In the end, they sat on the couch watching *Reach for the Stars*. A film about a robot alien girl who ended up dating a cute milk cow-boy who just wished to be human.

"Those are some fat tits on that dude. I thought he would be a bull. Why a heifer?" Hide asked.

"What's that? Hey, why is that house that colour? It is so ugly."

"This girl is like 4 out of 10. Looks wise. Even makeup-crusted hags have better appeal. This guy's gotta have better standards."

"Is this gonna be a musical, Loulou? What genre? Let me guess. Punk rock cus the current track is very punk rock."

"Loulou! What happened?"

Hide's questions and chatter started only ten minutes into the film.

"Um, it has a few songs," Loukas replied as he tried to pay attention to the movie. He could not help but glance at Hide's face, a beautiful thing, especially the way his thick, messy brows knitted when he was in thought.

"Ouch, that's gotta hurt crashing into a girl, but he should have kept his eyes on the road." Hide's chatter continued.

Maybe it was because Loukas had seen the film a million times already, but he could not exactly get annoyed with Hide's questions.

The little goat was simply a talkative man, and it was nice having something other than his thoughts speaking back to him for once.

It did not take long for Loukas to notice how close Hide was to him. The little goat-man's hand was on his thigh, forever tapping to make his next quip. Even after what had just occurred, he still was not afraid to be close to him.

"Oh shit, Loulou, this dipshit looks like my ex. A heartless bitch."

Loukas blinked when Hide mentioned that.

Oh yeah, Hide dates other people. Many other people.

Hide likes men, too.

Loukas bit down on his lip under the blue light of the television. He asked, "H-hey when did . . . did you . . . realise you liked guys?"

"What?" Hide tilted his head, taking his eyes off the screen.

"Oh, s-sorry if that's out of nowhere. I didn't mean—"

"Relax, damn it." Hide shrugged. "I'll say I kinda always knew that shit. It never really mattered to me, you know? I only like the best-looking people. Ugly people should have no rights. They take up too much space." Hide pulled his legs closer to himself and leaned back onto the soft seat cushions. "Maybe I can say my first dumbass crush was some guy at twelve years old.

"He was a dumb-fuck guy. Every chick in my school wanted to hold his stupid hand and kiss his dumb face. I was as brain-dead as them at the time and wrote him long, cringy secret admirer letters." He scrunched up his nose. "Ew, never again. Never do that to anyone. You might as well tape a 'Spit on Me' sign to your forehead."

"Oh."

"Okay, I said my piece. Now you tell me when you found out you were a fellow guy fancier." Hide added, "I figured you were in like . . . a month meeting you."

"H-how did you . . . I mean now, I guess, but . . ." Loukas did not know how to even answer that question.

He had only figured that out a few months ago, anyway. How could Hide have known so quickly?

"Bwahaha!"

Hide's laughter overpowered whatever romantic moment on screen.

"Your taste in shit-full of dull-nothing girls with kinda hot guys was a

CHAPTER 14

dead giveaway, even if I didn't notice until now. If I didn't get it within a month, I would have been blind, deaf, and dumb." Hide smiled. "Plus general vibes. I wouldn't have helped you jerk it on the phone if I thought you were completely straight."

Loukas wondered how obvious it had been. He knew if his family had known, it would not go down so well.

Did any of them suspect that?

Maybe his brother, but it had been so long since they had time to be with each other in person. His uncle had tried to get him into more masculine hobbies such as hunting before . . .

Maybe he knew.

"So you're gonna tell me?"

"H-huh?"

Hide rolled his eyes. "Ass-hat, I told mine. Now what's your first 'I want dick' moment?"

No way in hell was Loukas going to say Hide was his realisation.

But . . .

Now that Loukas thought about it, during his teen years, when his first kisses were dull, he remembered a person he just wanted to be around, despite the man's dismissal.

He truly was a degenerate.

"My . . . uncle."

Hide gave him a confused look, and it seemed he was about to say something before he held his tongue. "Oh, I see. Uh, I guess you win the odd crushes game."

Why didn't he hate him?

"You mentioned that you admired him a lot, right?" Hide asked. It was as if he genuinely wanted to know more about him.

But why? Why didn't he shame him?

Loukas' eyes were on the floor. "Yeah, I did . . . He was the first man I fantasised about. I know it's . . ."

Loukas felt a finger press against his nose, and Hide said, "I see. Your first taste was being a good boy to some old man. Daddy's boy?"

Hide cackled as Loukas buried his face in his hands. Of course, this would happen.

But why don't you hate me?

"Please don't say that," Loukas stammered.

Instead of rejection, what he had was Hide's interest. He did not pull away or call him names. Hide seemed to ponder what it all meant.

"How old was he, though?" Hide asked.

"Um . . . I think forty-something at the time?"

Hide looked like he sucked on a lemon and said, "Ew, that's an old man. Get some standards."

"I-I have standards!"

"For whom? Retirees?"

"N-no."

"Planning to hook up at the local nursing home?"

"Hide!"

"Loulou, are you secretly two old men in a trench coat?"

They laughed at the absurdity of it all. Hide kept up his teasing, and Loukas was not even sure if they were watching the movie Ass-hat with how much they were laughing.

Hide accepted him.

There had to be a catch.

There had to be something he was missing.

This was too good to be true.

"Hide?"

He could not take it any more.

"Boo, this film is boring. Action-packed sci-fi, my ass. Bet you think so too," Hide teased.

"Hide, I've been following you home for the entire summer."

"What?"

He had to end it.

He could not let Hide not know what he was, lie and pretend to be something he was not.

Loukas took a deep breath and told him, "This whole summer, I killed too

CHAPTER 14

many people. Each time I got so turned on during it. One p-person, I used his eye socket to put my penis in after he died. Each one I buried once I was done. Every single time I enjoyed it."

"Wait, wait," Hide interrupted, "Just, be honest with me here. Did. . . . Was there anyone making you do all that? Or forcing you? Anyone at all?"

Loukas was puzzled by those questions. The beast-kin had strange stern seriousness to him as if he was expecting a specific sort of answer. But why? Loukas thoughts then went to Xander and a feeling of nausea crept over him, especially towards their last interactions.

Could he even call any of what was done forced? He didn't even put in an ounce of resistance and as much as it sickens him, it felt comfortingly familiar. He had control over it all at the end of the day, and could have left at any point, but he didn't. He chose to stay and will choose again if Xander offered another opportunity to make him his star. Hence Loukas answered with, "No, No one forced anything."

Hide looked like he was about to say something else before he closed his mouth again and sighed.

Loukas then stared into his ceiling light and added, "No . . . I don't feel sorry that I killed them. I'm more sorry I could not resist it."

He said it.

He finally said it.

Hide stared at him. His ears were flat against his head.

Run.

Run far away.

This is who I am.

You despise me now?

Of course you do. Hate me until I die.

Tell me you wish I'd die.

"If you think I'm gonna run away because of that, you might be actually dumb as fuck," Hide spat out.

Loukas lifted his gaze to Hide. He noticed the goat's fist was in a tight ball, and his eyes were on fire.

Hide grabbed Loukas by his necklace. "I don't care what you are, but I'm not leaving you alone just like that. I'm saying this shit now. Loulou, you better not make me repeat myself. I'm staying whether you like it or not."

Hide's hand shook, and his gaze was harsh and filled with what Loukas fantasised about for so long.

Parental concern.

Loukas loved Hide.

Loukas loved Hide more than anything in this world.

Against his better judgement, he embraced the man. The goat let out a yelp, but Loukas ignored it, holding the man's small body against his own.

"Hide . . . can we stay like this?" he asked softly and hoped this never disappeared.

The goat ran his hand over Loukas' back and replied, "Of course, baby, as long as you want."

"I love you . . . I love you so much."

Loukas said those words over and over again. Not caring how repetitive it sounded as he rocked against Hide's body.

He lowered his eyelids, tired from the emotional tension that he had been bottling up for a long time.

He heard Hide's simple reply to his confession.

"I know, Loulou . . . I know."

Loukas was not disappointed since reciprocation was not important to him. He just wanted acknowledgement and to be, for once, not the worst part of another person's existence. He wasn't a burden born that even his mother regretted carrying, nor a monster. To Hide he was just a person in his life and for now, that was all he needed to hear from the man.

He was happy.

CHAPTER 15

For the first time in months, Loukas had a peaceful sleep.

It was devoid of his usual nightmares and fitful terrors. Instead, his body relaxed and everything felt so right and at peace.

For once, he felt no guilt, shame, or hatred. He was content with what he had, and he did not wish for anything else. He was happy.

When he opened his eyes again, he was unsurprised to find himself still on the couch. He had emotionally prepared for and expected his visitor to have left, just like before. The presence of an unusually heavy body on his chest, breathing softly, shattered that expectation. All confirming that Hide kept his promise.

He stayed with him.

Loukas could not help but smile when his eyes drifted over the small man's body.

Hide stayed for him.

Xander may have taught him about his uncontrollable interest, but Hide still stayed after learning about it. That was more than what Loukas deserved, yet he still received it.

On his chest was the little goat where he could admire every part of it in silence.

The snuggle Hide had on Loukas' shirt with his fists was charming, and the way his brow knitted in his sleep made Loukas worry about what dreams he was having. Loukas was unsure whether he should move or stay.

Hide nuzzled into his chest, with long hair falling over his neck, his floppy ears twitching, and his tail lazily wagging to his soft breaths. His hips moved a bit before going still, and Loukas' internal conflict about moving or staying grew.

He sniffed the air and noticed that Hide seemed to ooze a sickly sweet scent. So sweet it made Loukas' mind feel hazy.

His stomach made it hard not to notice how tasty he smelt.

Did he always smell this way?

Maybe the scent was when beast-kins went into rut. Was that possible? He should ask some day. Or maybe he had always smelt so desirable and only now that Loukas had just a small taste he needed more.

Hide's face was so peaceful, one would mistake him for a cute creature of innocence.

That scent was perfect.

Loukas moved his hand over Hide's face, brushing his hair away from his lidded eyes. Hide did not like to have his ears touched, so Loukas kept his hands away from there out of respect. Loukas pressed his face into the older man's body and sniffed him, allowing his beast-kin's odour to roll off his body even stronger.

Hide would never let Loukas do this to him if he was awake, but Loukas did not care. He wanted to consume Hide's scent, his very being.

Loukas nuzzled into his neck, sliding a wet tongue over his skin.

Why was he so perfect?

Hide accepted the monster he was, even after Loukas told him what he did.

Hide was too cute and beyond his dreams; the idea of breaking his legs to stop him from leaving was so tempting.

Hide was his and his alone.

He held Hide, licking his neck, allowing his tongue to gently caress every inch of skin. The thrill of getting caught sent a prickle through Loukas' core. What if Hide still accepted him like this?

On some level, Loukas was aware he would plunge into guilt once Hide woke up, but for now, he allowed himself to indulge in his obsessive fixation.

CHAPTER 15

Loukas went to Hide's ear. He wanted to tell him his own secret affirmation, knowing very well Hide could not hear him.

It was a declaration more to himself when Loukas whispered, "Mine."

Those fluffy ears perked up and flicked a bit. Loukas smiled. The guilt never came to him, and his treasure remained.

Hide will be mine.

Maybe someday, Loukas would finally be nothing more than rot and full of maggots, and Hide would be the same. Infected with his illness and spend their forever laughing.

Now to spoil his little goat with the same disease as himself.

Thank you so much for reading. When you're a brand-new author, it can be hard to convince people that your first book of a series is any good. If you enjoyed Listeriosis, it would mean the world to me if you would take a moment to leave a review. If you didn't know already this book is a sequel to the first book in the Hounding Prey series Monilnia. You can read where its all started.

And for updates and news on future books in the series and advance copies please it would mean so much if you sign up to F. Mints Newsletter as well as a special newsletter exclusive bonus story.

Enjoy this book? Don't be afraid to check out Your Cup of Absinthe for another MM story this time in a Victorian setting. Want something quick and sexy? Check out this short that takes place in the same universe, Piggy.

-Mints

Handling Prey Book Two: LISTEROSIS

CHAPTER 15

About the Author

A little guy who just wants to tell uncomfortable stories. A cat person who hopes to one day form an all cat run publishing house.

You can connect with me on:
 https://darkfeaturescoven.godaddysites.com

Subscribe to my newsletter:
 https://subscribepage.io/Fmints

Printed in the USA
CPSIA information can be obtained
at www.ICGtesting.com
LVHW031119301124
797922LV00009B/576